BHOOTA GAPPA

Part 2

The Death of a Beloved & 14 Other Short Horror Stories (Just Utter Horror)

PRATIKSHA MISRA

INDIA • SINGAPORE • MALAYSIA

Another "Bhoota Gappa"

"Sweating the last drop,
He drags himself,
To the corner of the shelf.
The heart beats faster,
Getting short of breath.
He must fight death,
Unknowingly alive.
After a deep dark dive.
The room is getting darker,
But that doesn't scare the lurker.
If there isn't a tall shadow.
On the wall that swallows.
Making it hard to see,
Making it harder to break free.
His bruised knee,
Urging to flee.
As his body trembles.
Tightening the shake within,
Finding a way to a never-ending win,
There lies the key,
Opening to the vast sea.
Emptiness wallows,
Shouting gets unheard.
Until ears ask him to stop being absurd.
There's a leap.
That gets steep.
A final weep.
With sunset running away,

The moon shines,
Glistening to his cry for a while,
With a sudden stop,
Fear ceases,
His breathing eases."

CONTENTS

The Main Characters in Shikaar-Nagar

▶ Contents ◀

The Story Till Now: Azagka: The Dawn of Fear

"2 Min Horror Stories" by Justutter Horror

▶ CONTENTS ◀

From "2 Min Horror Stories" Collection – Stories from Readers

INTRODUCTION

"Bhoota Gappa", means "Ghost Stories", in Odia language, and that's my native language from the land of Lord Jagannath where I come from, called Odisha, an eastern state of India famous for its culture, food, handicraft and temples. If you haven't read the first part, please begin your journey by grabbing your copy of "**Bhoota Gappa -Part 1**", as I introduce the characters in the first part of the series.

"**Bhoota Gappa - Part 2**", is the name of this book, that continues the gripping horror anthology series by *JustUtter*, weaving a chilling and emotionally charged narrative like never before. This installment delves into four parallel timelines, where characters exist, merge, vanish, or fade away, creating a labyrinth of interconnected fates.

At the heart of the story is AzaGka and her seven siblings, caught in a harrowing battle against a dark curse that threatens to unravel their world. Joined by their father, Ashvath, they navigate haunting emotional flashbacks that reveal the origins of their downfall and the pain of losing a loved one up close.

For the first time, this collection features short horror stories submitted by *JustUtter* readers—raw, untold tales of emotional upheaval and eerie encounters from across India. These 14 stories intertwine with the main narrative, intensifying the mystery and immersing readers in the cursed realm of Shikaar-Nagar.

Prepare to embark on a bone-chilling journey where horror meets healing, as the characters fight to bring peace to the fractured soul of one who has faced death's shadow too intimately. **"Bhoota Gappa - Part 2"** will leave you questioning reality and craving resolution in the face of darkness.

All the stories and characters in this book are imaginary and were personal experiences shared by individuals. Any resemblance to anyone else's experiences or life events are purely coincidental.

ACKNOWLEDGEMENT

I dedicate this book to my late father who was not only my father, but also a friend, philosopher and the best guide one can ever wish for. He was the one who inspired me to read books every day and to keep writing articles, stories, poems, whenever I can.

My father, who himself was a writer, until his last breath shared his numerous experiences, where he bravely encountered his fear, by creating unusual stories out of it, that made him an excellent conversationist. Never in his entire lifetime did he need to make gossip a chapter to strike a chord with the different kinds of people he met through the various stages from childhood to adulthood. He strongly believed that stories and books contain the power to make each other grow their inner circle of attaining mental peace.

"There is art hidden behind the science of knowing."

– JustUtter

THE MAIN CHARACTERS IN SHIKAAR-NAGAR

Introduction to Shikaar-Nagar, Odisha

Shikaar-Nagar is a suburb in Odisha steeped in ancient traditions and shrouded in mystery—a place where dense, impenetrable forests embrace a community bound by orthodox beliefs and dark legends. Here, the boundaries between the living and the dead blur, as if the very soil is haunted by the echoes of forgotten rituals and unresolved curses. In this cursed land, a parallel dark world has taken root alongside everyday life.

Ruthless murders, chaotic violence, and even child slaughter have left indelible marks on Shikaar-Nagar's history. Animal sacrifices and forbidden black magic have long been the desperate tools used by those seeking to appease or control the unseen forces that lurk in the shadows. The very air hums with a grim reminder: until the curse is lifted at its root, the dwellers of Shikaar-Nagar remain trapped, unable to escape the malignant destiny that binds them.

Legend has it that ancient folklore permeates every corner of this land. Stories passed down through generations speak of deities and demons, of celestial battles and earthly betrayals. The forests, thick and mysterious, are said to be the realm of forgotten gods and vengeful spirits. It is here that the dead mingle freely with the living, their silent presences etched into the fabric of daily existence. Every rustle of leaves, every shadow cast by the ancient trees, whispers of a past marred by curses and sacrifices.

For those brave enough to stand against this tide of darkness, vigilance is not an option - it is a necessity. In the first part of the *Bhoota Gappa* series, we were introduced to AzaGka, a determined investigator with a knack for unraveling spectral mysteries, and Ekaksh, a resolute cop whose unyielding spirit challenges both mortal criminals and paranormal terrors. In Shikaar-Nagar, their quest is relentless: to uncover the sinister truths behind the violence and horror that have become the dark heartbeat of their community, and to protect what little hope remains among the living.

AzaGka and Ekaksh patrol the eerie streets and hidden corners of Shikaar-Nagar, where the curse has woven a legacy of despair. Here, every soul—whether in flesh or spirit— bears the weight of an inescapable, long-forgotten legacy. In this land, the dead are as much a part of the landscape as the living. Ghosts of the past mingle with present terrors, and every whisper of wind through the dense forests serves as a reminder that the ancient curse continues to claim lives.

Welcome to Shikaar-Nagar—a realm where ancient folklore and modern nightmare collide, where every step taken is a battle against the darkness, and where the survival of its people hinges on confronting a destiny written in the shadows.

AZAGKA

The Unyielding Beacon of Shikaar-Nagar

In the cursed, shadowed realm of Shikaar-Nagar, where ancient traditions mingle with modern terror and every corner whispers of dark rituals and unresolved curses, one woman rises as a pillar of strength and defiance. AzaGka is not just an investigator or a fighter - she is a force of nature. At 42, with a spirit tempered by loss and hardship, she embodies the fighting fire that refuses to be snuffed out, even in a land where women are too often branded as witches and stripped of their dignity.

Born in a suburb of Odisha where dense, impenetrable forests hide more than just nature's secrets, AzaGka lost her mother at an early age. Though her father is lost beyond the realm of existence, his presence lingers in the other world—a spectral guide she meets when unraveling the dark mysteries that plague her homeland. Her life is a precarious dance between the light of knowledge and the devouring depths of the unknown.

AzaGka's journey began in an orphanage, a sanctuary for six other siblings who, like her, were plucked from the darkest corners of a scarred past. Rather than succumbing to despair, they forged an unbreakable bond – a thread of darkness that paradoxically became a lifeline. Together, they stand as a makeshift family, a testament to resilience in a place where every day is a battle against ghouls, spirits, and the remnants of ancient curses.

By day, AzaGka is a respected professor at the Shikaar-Nagar Institute for Mad Scientists - a haven for those who dare to explore the depths of human psychology and the realm beyond the dead. In the lecture halls, she challenges her students to question what lies beneath the surface of reality, pushing them to confront the sinister forces that lurk in every shadow of Shikaar-Nagar. Her wisdom, born of suffering and triumph, makes her a beacon of hope for those who have been marked and marginalized by a society steeped in superstition.

Yet, her academic role is only a fraction of her identity. In the perilous nights of Shikaar-Nagar, where ruthless murders, chaotic violence, and forbidden black magic threaten to tear the community apart, AzaGka transforms into a lone warrior. With unwavering resolve, she ventures into the darkest alleys and deepest forests, unearthing secrets that many would rather leave buried. In her battles against malevolent forces, she is a relentless investigator and a savior—a rare force of nature fighting back against the tide of despair.

AzaGka's story is woven into the fabric of the *Bhoota Gappa* series—a seven-part saga that chronicles her relentless quest to break the ancient curse gripping Shikaar-Nagar. In a land where the dead walk as freely as the living, her struggle is not only for her own redemption but for the very soul of a community mired in fear and superstition.

Join her as she stands tall against predators of both flesh and spirit—a living testament that even in the darkest realms, a spark of defiant light can ignite a revolution. AzaGka is the embodiment of strength, intellect, and unwavering hope in a world that seeks to snuff out both.

ASHVATH

The Phantom Protector of Shikaar-Nagar

Ashvath is a man shaped by tragedy and steeped in the dark lore of Shikaar-Nagar. Once a proud, handsome figure—a tall, fair-complexioned man with a striking bushy black moustache, he was born into an orthodox family whose legacy was defined by both honor and hidden sorrow. His father, a respected electrical engineer at the Indian Railways, instilled in him the secrets of a land where even technology and tradition intermingled with the supernatural. Yet, that same father bore a painful history of forbidden love - a man forced into a marriage he never desired because of societal scorn, an echo of pain that has rippled through generations.

In his youth, Ashvath's world was one of wonder and routine visits to bustling railway stations, where the modern pulse of the city met the timeless rhythm of the rails. But darkness lurked in the depths of the forests surrounding Shikaar-Nagar. His younger sister, Avannya, fell victim to a monstrous presence hidden among the ancient trees, and his mother, devastated by the cruelty of fate, withdrew into the very forest that whispered with secrets and curses.

As an adult, Ashvath worked tirelessly at the steel plant, striving to secure a future for his beloved daughter, AzaGka. Yet fate dealt him another cruel blow: a tragic accident claimed the life of his wife, shattering the last vestige of his mortal existence. In that moment, Ashvath's spirit was torn between worlds. He became lost in the realm of the dead, ultimately emerging as a werewolf—a spectral guardian who straddles the border between life and oblivion.

Now, in his ghostly lupine form, Ashvath defies his fate by returning to guide his daughter. Despite his existence in a shadowy realm, his presence is as potent as ever. He aids AzaGka in her relentless investigations into the ancient folklore and eldritch horrors that have long tormented Shikaar-Nagar. Drawing from his own life's tragedies and the haunting lessons passed down by his father, Ashvath provides her with the wisdom of a man who has known both deep love and bitter loss.

Ashvath's legacy is one of duality—torn between the world of the living and the spectral domain of the dead. He embodies the strength and resilience of a broken lineage, offering his daughter the freedom to embrace her identity and to belong, despite the curse that hangs heavy over their land. In every whisper of the wind and every shadow that flits through Shikaar-Nagar's dense forests, his protective howl resonates—a reminder that even in darkness, love and hope endure.

ASMI & ARIT

The Scars and Sparks of Bhoota Gappa

At their grandparents' crumbling estate in Shikaar-Nagar, a memory seared into their young minds forever changed the course of their lives. It was there that Arit, a 15-year-old boy with a genius spark, and Asmi, an 11-year-old girl with a tender, naturalistic soul, witnessed a chilling event: a mysterious lady in white emerged from the mists of their ancestral home. Her spectral presence was as mesmerizing as it was terrifying. In a moment of grim retribution, she murdered their next-door neighbor, a man who had once taken her life and then, with ritualistic precision, buried her own remains in the old pond behind the house. This grotesque tableau unfolded against the backdrop of a family already shattered by a religious cult war that had claimed their parents at an early age.

For Arit, this encounter ignited a relentless quest for answers. Scarred by loss yet fueled by an insatiable curiosity, he became the mastermind behind discovering hidden pathways and inventing ingenious methods to control the dark hazards lurking in Shikaar-Nagar. The memory of that tragic night—of spectral vengeance and the twisted interplay of life and death—became the driving force behind his determination to tame the supernatural. Arit's mind, ever restless, now seeks to chart the unknown, turning his pain into a weapon against the darkness that threatens to consume their world.

In contrast, Asmi found solace and strength in the natural rhythms of life. While following in Arit's adventurous footsteps, she chose a path of organic magic and empathy. The haunting images of the lady in white and the blood-stained pond awakened in her a deep connection to the elements: earth, fire, water, and air, and to the hidden magical creatures that dwell in the fringes of reality, from gentle elves to elusive fairies and benevolent spirits. For Asmi, nature is a healing balm and a reservoir of hope, offering guidance and protection where human institutions have failed. Her creativity blossoms into art and ritual, a quiet counterbalance to the chaos around her.

Together, Arit and Asmi are the living embodiment of resilience in Shikaar-Nagar—a land where the boundaries between the living and the dead are as thin as a whisper. In the wake of their parents' tragic loss and the ensuing family conflict, they have forged an unbreakable bond, clinging to each other as their sole remnant of family. Their shared adventure, chronicled in *Bhoota Gappa,* is a testament to the indomitable spirit of those who, though marked by tragedy, rise to fight the encroaching darkness. They stand ready to support AzaGka and protect their newly found siblings, driven by an unwavering belief that the strength of family can heal even the deepest wounds inflicted by ancient curses and unspeakable horrors.

In Shikaar-Nagar, where every shadow holds a secret and every rustle in the forest carries the weight of lost legends, Arit's innovative mind and Asmi's naturalistic soul shine as beacons of hope, a promise that even in a world steeped in death and despair, the light of determination and unity will endure.

ABHAYA

The Haunted Seer of Shikaar-Nagar

Abhaya is a 25-year-old woman whose life has been etched with sorrow and supernatural gifts. Having lost her parents in a devastating fire in Mumbai, a tragedy that scarred her soul, she carries a deep loneliness, tempered by a mysterious power that sets her apart. From an early age, Abhaya discovered that the veil between the living and the dead was thinner for her. With the uncanny ability to read the minds of evil spirits and summon them using the ancient art of planchette, she has become both a reluctant seer and a target of fate in a world steeped in dark folklore.

Her life in Mumbai was a constant battle against haunting memories. One particularly dreadful night still lingers in her recollection: After a late meeting, she rushed to the nearly deserted train station at 2:00 AM, desperate to catch the last local back to her modest apartment. The normally bustling station was eerily silent, and as she stepped outside, a distant, collective scream of women shattered the stillness. Every instinct screamed danger. Yet, in that fearful moment, she found solace in her transgender friend, Radha—whose warmth and kindness had been a lifeline through Mumbai's torrential rains, power outages, and even in the wake of the blasts that took her parents. Radha's compassionate presence, marked by simple gestures, like, a shared 10-rupee note and a heartfelt blessing, provided Abhaya with the strength to face another dark chapter in her life.

That fateful night unfolded into a surreal, spine-chilling encounter. As Abhaya walked under a bridge on a moonless Amavasya night, she witnessed a group of mysterious women gathered in a circle, their strange ritualistic feast inexplicably luring the attention of unseen forces. When a frail, seated woman with a piercing gaze approached, followed by chaotic, shrill screams, Abhaya's heart pounded in terror. It was then that the spectral figures, like a flock of crows, took flight into the dark sky, a manifestation of the malevolent spirits she was uniquely sensitive to. Radha's timely intervention and wise words, that these were evil entities feeding on the remnants of death, reminded Abhaya of the precarious balance she maintained between the realms of the living and the dead.

Despite her profound abilities, Abhaya is a paradox of fragility and strength. She yearns to escape the darkness that clings to her, yet the very power that marks her as a witch in the eyes of a superstitious world also ties her inescapably to it. Her gift of communing with and commanding the evil spirits comes at a steep personal cost—one that isolates her from a society that is quick to judge and ostracize.

Now, as part of the broken yet unyielding family of Shikaar-Nagar, Abhaya stands alongside her siblings, each bearing their own scars from a turbulent past. In the labyrinthine alleys of this cursed land, where ancient curses and modern nightmares converge, Abhaya's prophetic insight is both a beacon of hope and a burden. Her inner struggle reflects the eternal conflict between light and darkness—a battle that defines not only her existence but also the fate of Shikaar-Nagar itself.

In the *Bhoota Gappa* series, Abhaya's character is a poignant reminder of how tragedy can forge an unexpected strength. Amid the chaos of ruthless murders, dark magic, and spectral terrors, she endures—fighting against the shadows, seeking redemption, and striving to protect the delicate bonds of family that, despite being pieced together from the fragments of loss, still stand defiant in a world where the dead walk as freely as the living.

EKAKSH

The Unyielding Sentinel of Shikaar-Nagar

Ekaksh is a towering 45-year-old cop in Shikaar-Nagar—a man whose very presence seems carved out of the hardships of a brutal world. With his dark, imposing figure, a thick, bushy moustache, and an unmistakable air of authority forged from an army background, Ekaksh stands as a living testament to survival in a land riddled with ancient curses and modern horrors.

From his early days in an orphanage—a time when even a kind, guiding figure offered a glimmer of hope, Ekaksh learned that mercy and strength must coexist in a world that often shows none. His formative years were marred by loss, as he witnessed the ruthless killing of Naxals and saw his closest comrades fall in vicious attacks, leaving indelible scars on his soul. Those painful memories now drive his relentless pursuit of justice and his unwavering commitment to protect the innocent.

In the cursed realm of Shikaar-Nagar, where the living share the stage with the dead, Ekaksh has earned an almost mythical reputation. Whispers tell of an eerie entourage of zombies, spectral followers who seem to arise from the very shadows of his past battles, marking his every step. These undead allies, whether a supernatural manifestation of his inner demons or a grim reflection of the world's cruelty, serve as a constant reminder of the price he has paid for his convictions.

Yet, beyond the hardened cop and battle-scarred warrior, Ekaksh has discovered a chance at family, a gift bestowed upon him by Ram. In this broken, cursed land, Ram has given him the opportunity to build a familial bond with those who had once been mere strangers. Among these bonds, none is more profound than the one he shares with AzaGka. Acting as both a protective elder brother and a relentless mentor, Ekaksh pushes AzaGka to embrace fearlessness. He commands her in the only way he knows how, firmly and with unwavering determination, guiding her as they solve mysteries and confront monstrous forces together.

Ekaksh's relationship with his siblings is a testament to resilience and hope amid despair. His protective nature is balanced by his insistence that every child in Shikaar-Nagar learns to survive in a ruthless world, a world where mortal combat and mental fortitude are necessary for survival. With every case they crack and every dark secret they unearth, Ekaksh and AzaGka's bond grows stronger, symbolizing the fragile yet unyielding unity of a family forged in tragedy.

In the *Bhoota Gappa* series, Ekaksh's story is one of survival, redemption, and the transformative power of family. He is not merely a soldier against darkness but also a beacon for those who have been abandoned by fate. Through his guidance and the strength of his convictions, he ensures that even in a land haunted by curses and spectral terrors, hope can still flourish and that every child, every soul, learns to rise against the encroaching shadows.

VIANSH

The Unbound Spirit of Shikaar-Nagar

Viansh, the youngest sibling of AzaGka, is a 20-year-old force of nature, a living spark in the darkened tapestry of Shikaar-Nagar. Born under turbulent circumstances, he was abandoned outside a temple and christened "Viansh," meaning "part of God," a name that would come to define his extraordinary destiny. Raised in an orphanage among six other siblings, Viansh quickly learned that family isn't always defined by blood, but by the bonds forged through shared struggle and resilience.

From a young age, Viansh exhibited a wild, indomitable energy that set him apart. His childhood, filled with nightmares so vivid, they left him bruised in the morning, revealed a deeper connection to a world beyond mundane. These dreams; battles, chases by wild animals, and surreal encounters with shadowy figures, hinted at the latent power within him. As he grew older, Viansh discovered his unique gift: the ability to shape-shift in the parallel world, slipping seamlessly into the forms of animals to traverse the wild, untamed landscapes of Shikaar-Nagar. This power not only made him an invaluable scout in their dangerous, cursed land, but also a symbol of freedom and transformation.

Viansh's charm is as undeniable as his supernatural talents. With a magnetic personality and a playful smile, he easily captures the attention of those around him. His flirtatious nature and open bisexuality allow him to move fluidly between worlds and relationships, unbound by traditional norms. For him, life is a thrilling adventure, and every encounter, whether with a mischievous spirit or a potential lover, fuels his relentless zest for life.

One of his most defining memories occurred on a dark, stormy night when, walking home on foot because his cycle was in the repair shop, he sensed a presence lurking behind him. In that moment, the streetlights flickered, and his heart pounded as he encountered a mysterious, bat-like shadow with bloodshot eyes clinging to a banyan tree. Though fear gripped him, it was that very experience that solidified his resolve to confront the unknown head-on, a testament to his spirit of valor and curiosity.

Viansh's boundless energy and transformative abilities make him an indispensable ally in the fight against the dark forces that plague Shikaar-Nagar. Whether he's morphing into a stealthy animal to gather crucial intelligence or charming friends and foes alike with his magnetic presence, Viansh embodies the wild, untamed essence of a land where the living and the dead walk side by side.

As the best and most resilient of AzaGka's siblings, Viansh is not just a survivor, he is a beacon of hope and a reminder that even in the face of ancient curses and relentless darkness, the human spirit can remain free, fierce, and ever transformative. His story is one of unyielding adventure and self-discovery—a vibrant thread in the complex fabric of the *Bhoota Gappa* saga, where every shadow holds a secret, and every soul yearns to be seen.

SHLOKA

The Silent Oracle

Shloka is the quiet heart of Shikaar-Nagar, a woman whose silence speaks louder than words ever could. Having lost her voice in a tragic accident that claimed both her parents, she carries a deep, unspoken grief, a void filled, paradoxically, by a remarkable gift. While she can no longer speaks, Shloka has the uncanny ability to hear what lies beyond the visible world. The whispers of unseen spirits, the murmurs of fate, and even echoes of the future resonate in her mind, guiding her in ways that defy ordinary understanding.

One memory that haunts her, and has shaped her destiny, dates back to a moonlit night in Kandarpur, a small village in Derabish Tehsil, Kendrapara district of Odisha. It was just past midnight, and a power outage had plunged the village into deep, unnerving darkness. Shloka lay on a cot on her grandparents' terrace, the tall coconut trees outside silently observing the night. Amid the stillness, she heard the distant jingle of bangles, a sound that seemed out of place and time. Venturing to the edge of the terrace, she caught a glimpse of a mysterious woman moving in the darkness, her bangles chiming like a spectral lullaby. This eerie encounter, along with the unsettling atmosphere of that night, filled with ominous sounds and inexplicable occurrences, etched itself into Shloka's memory, marking the beginning of her ability to perceive the hidden voices of the world.

Now, as the best friend of AzaGka, Shloka's silent strength and prophetic visions have become invaluable. Though her voice was taken from her, her inner ear listens to the fate that unfolds around her. She senses dangers long before they strike and understands the subtle shifts in destiny that most cannot fathom. Her presence is a constant, reassuring reminder that even in silence, one can communicate volumes through glances, gestures, and the deep, knowing look in her eyes.

Shloka's unique power of hearing the future and the voices of unseen realms makes her both a blessing and a burden. She carries the weight of tragic loss, yet her gift offers hope and guidance in the cursed land of Shikaar-Nagar. Amid ruthless darkness, her silent oracle-like insight is a beacon that helps steer her loved ones away from impending calamity. Even though she cannot speak, her inner voice resounds with the wisdom of the ages, urging those around her to heed the warnings of the unseen and prepare for what lies ahead.

In the intricate tapestry of the *Bhoota Gappa* series, Shloka's character is a testament to resilience and the paradox of silence. Marked by tragedy yet empowered by an extraordinary gift, she stands as a quiet guardian—a living bridge between the known and the mysterious, forever listening to the unspoken secrets of a world where the future is whispered on the wind.

RAM

The Guardian of Shadows and Lost Souls

Ram is a man whose past is as intricate as the dark legends of Shikaar-Nagar. Once a formidable practitioner of black magic and a powerful tantrik ("Sorcerer"), he now devotes himself to the orphanage that shelters AzaGka and her siblings, a place where hope struggles to survive amid ancient curses and modern horrors.

A close friend of Ashvath since their college days, Ram's bond with him runs deep. When Ram lost his beloved wife, Tiksha, and was left with a 9-year-old AzaGka to care for, at a time when Ashvath had already begun his spectral existence as a werewolf in the realm of the dead, Ram reached out to his longtime friend for help. Despite Ashvath's physical absence in the world of the living, his guidance and protective spirit have continued to shape AzaGka's journey. Their shared past, marked by intense struggles and the unyielding fight against supernatural forces, has forged an unbreakable alliance that spans both the mortal plane and the alter-verse.

Tiksha, Ram's late wife, has not truly departed. In the mysterious corridors of the alter-verse, she endures as a spectral guardian with formidable mystical powers. An ardent scientist of witchcraft, Tiksha possesses a profound understanding of the brain's chemical intensity and the ways in which spirits manipulate it. Time and again, she visits Ram, offering her ethereal support to him, AzaGka, and the beleaguered community of Shikaar-Nagar, ensuring that even in the absence of physical presence, her love and guidance continue to light the path for those trapped in darkness.

Ram's life is defined by contrasts: once a master of the arcane arts alongside his devoted partner, Daksh, he has since set aside the fervor of his old cultic practices. Now, his power lies not in grand rituals, but in his steadfast commitment to nurturing a family forged out of shared loss and relentless hope. His journey from a grief-stricken widower to the compassionate caregiver of the orphanage is a testament to his indomitable spirit and his belief in the strength of kinship, whether bound by blood or by destiny.

As the caregiver of AzaGka and her siblings, Ram is both a mentor and a protector. He instills in them the resilience required to survive in a ruthless world, where ancient curses and the specters of the past linger at every corner. With Ashvath's spectral counsel guiding them from beyond and Tiksha's mysterious, recurring presence in the alter-verse lending them mystical support, Ram stands as a beacon of hope in Shikaar-Nagar, a land where the living and the dead share the same dark streets, and every soul clings to the promise of redemption in the midst of overwhelming despair.

DAKSH

The Haunted Redeemer of Shikaar-Nagar

Daksh is a man whose journey through darkness has forged him into a reluctant healer of the supernatural. Once a troubled youth with an unyielding affinity for men, Daksh was barred from school and education by his own parents due to his open gay identity. This rejection plunged him into a dark underworld of drugs and crime, a tumultuous period that left deep emotional scars and nearly consumed his spirit.

The turning point in Daksh's life came unexpectedly at the funeral of his estranged wife, where he reconnected with Ram, a steadfast friend and former partner of Ashvath. In that moment of shared grief and loss, Ram's compassion and unwavering resolve sparked in Daksh a desire to reclaim his life and find a purpose beyond the chaos of his past. Ram, recognizing the latent strength within him, pulled Daksh into the mysterious realm of managing the dead, guiding him to channel his profound empathy into becoming a sort of "dead psychiatrist." Daksh now uses his unique ability to understand and soothe the tormented spirits who seek death and revenge, aiding those who feel wronged by the living.

Though his role in the current series is understated, Daksh's evolution from a lost soul in the clutches of darkness to a guardian of haunted spirits hints at a deeper, more significant future. His journey is one of redemption and transformation—a testament to the power of love, resilience, and the possibility of healing even the most scarred hearts in Shikaar-Nagar. As the curse that haunts the land begins to unravel, Daksh is poised to become an indispensable ally in the battle for the betterment of his community, embodying the hope that even the most damaged souls can rise to mend the fabric of a cursed world.

ASHVATH'S MOTHER & FATHER

The Pillars of a Haunting Legacy

Ashvath's father was a striking figure—a tall, handsome man with a fair complexion and a bushy black moustache. Born into an orthodox family, he rose to become a respected electrical engineer at the Indian Railways. His life was a tapestry woven with routine and uncanny: on many late-night assignments, he encountered mysteries that defied logic. In one such fateful encounter, he crossed paths with a grim reaper, a spectral figure whose presence at deserted railway stations sparked both dread and fascination. Instead of recoiling in terror, his father found himself drawn into an unexpected friendship with this enigmatic entity. This eerie bond, forged in the cold shadows of the railways, offered him cryptic insights into the nature of life and death, a wisdom he would later pass on, shaping his guidance for his son, Ashvath.

In contrast, Ashvath's mother was a gentle yet steadfast presence, a dedicated high school science teacher whose rational mind provided balance to the family's mystique. Known for her nurturing spirit and keen intellect, she instilled in her children a respect for knowledge and reason. However, tragedy would test her resolve. When their younger daughter, Avannya, fell prey to a lurking monster in the deep, dark forest that fringed Shikaar-Nagar, her grief and inability to forgive fate drove her into seclusion. She withdrew from the outside world, seeking solace and perhaps a way to understand the inexplicable forces that had shattered their lives.

Together, Ashvath's parents embodied the paradox of their homeland, Shikaar-Nagar, a suburb adored for its reputable, well-rooted families, yet forever shadowed by ancient secrets and supernatural mysteries. Their contrasting paths one steeped in the arcane whispers of the railway's haunted nights and the other in the measured wisdom of science and education formed the foundation of a legacy that would echo through generations, influencing not only Ashvath's destiny but also the very soul of Shikaar Nagar.

AZAGKA'S MOTHER & GRANDMOTHER: DAHANA & ANALA

Dahana: The Fiery Empress of Shikaar-Nagar

Dahana, whose name means "Burning Fire," is a figure forged in the crucible of loss, power, and destiny. Born to Anala, a formidable widow whose life was marred by cruelty and superstition, Dahana inherited a legacy of fire and mysticism that would shape her destiny and the fate of Shikaar-Nagar.

Anala: The Inferno Matriarch

Anala's life was a testament to resilience in the face of injustice. After her husband died in a tragic accident, her in-laws tortured and blamed her for his death, branding her a witch. Forced to abandon her village, Anala roamed the woods with her four children, enduring days of starvation and despair. Seeking refuge, she took shelter in a cave where, amid solitude and suffering, she unlocked the secrets of multidimensional worlds.

In time, Anala mastered the art of controlling fire with devastating precision. Legends in Shikaar-Nagar speak of her taming a fearsome dragon named Jokha, lent to rulers to protect their vast treasures and of her command over other deadly beasts that haunted the cursed lands.

Dahana's Transformation and Rise:

When Dahana met Ashvath during their college days, she was a simple, unassuming girl with no apparent supernatural powers, entirely of the real world. Yet, the spark of her ancestral legacy was waiting to be ignited. Drawing on the potent, mind-controlling magic passed down from her mother, Dahana used her newfound abilities to captivate and win Ashvath's trust and love. Their union was unconventional, especially given Ashvath's earlier inclinations toward the same gender, but Dahana's compelling blend of vulnerability and latent power ultimately sealed their bond.

A Fiery and Possessive Love:

As their relationship deepened, Dahana's powers continued to grow. However, the same mystical gifts that had drawn Ashvath to her also fostered severe trust issues. Possessive and fiercely protective, she would scorch anyone who dared come too close to Ashvath, a reflection of her internal battles and the scars of her turbulent past. Even after giving birth to AzaGka, Dahana's struggle to balance love and control led to conflicts with her daughter, leaving a lasting imprint on their relationship.

The Tragic Fall:

For a time, despite the underlying tensions and the harsh realities of their cursed world, Dahana and Ashvath managed to hold their lives together. But fate, as it often does in Shikaar-Nagar, intervened with ruthless finality. In a sudden, mysterious attack emanating from the hidden realm, Dahana was killed. Her untimely demise shattered the fragile balance of her world, leaving Ashvath and AzaGka to grapple with the immense void of loss and the cascading effects of her absence.

Dahana's life is a tapestry of intense passion, raw power, and profound tragedy—a journey from humble beginnings to a state of fiery ascendancy, only to be cut short by forces beyond mortal control. Her legacy, however, burns on in the memories and battles of those she left behind, a blazing reminder of the transformative, often destructive, power of destiny in Shikaar-Nagar.

RAM'S WIFE – TIKSHA

The Eternal Healer of the Dark Realm

Tiksha is a beacon of love, honor, and resilience in the shadowed world of Shikaar-Nagar. As a respected Sanskrit teacher at the Dark Arts College, she carries an air of dignity and profound knowledge—a woman whose gentle grace and timeless wisdom instantly captured the heart of Ram. Their love story was one of instant connection and shared dreams, and for a while, they lived a blissful life marked by passion and mutual respect.

However, fate dealt them a cruel hand. Despite their deep love and harmonious life, the couple was cursed with the inability to have children, a void that gradually weighed on Tiksha's spirit. As the years passed, the absence of an heir left her increasingly worried and physically weakened, a sorrow that slowly chipped away at her once vibrant energy.

Yet even in death, Tiksha's legacy would not be extinguished. Through the dark arts that Ram mastered, he managed to preserve her essence, allowing her spirit to continue thriving in the realm of the dead. Transcending mortal limitations, Tiksha emerged in this spirited world as a formidable witch endowed with intense healing powers.

Her transformation was not one of loss but of rebirth, a metamorphosis that turned her grief into a profound gift for others.

Now, as the dark battles rage across Shikaar-Nagar, Tiksha stands as a steadfast guardian. She aids AzaGka, bolstering her with healing energy and guiding her through the treacherous labyrinth of curses and supernatural adversaries. Alongside Ashvath and the seven siblings, Tiksha's spectral presence is a source of comfort and strength, a reminder that even in a realm dominated by shadows, love and healing can light the way through every battle.

THE STORY TILL NOW: AZAGKA: THE DAWN OF FEAR

AzaGka, a 42-year-old professor and investigator, exists between academia and the supernatural. Born in *Shikaar Nagar*, a cursed land built over a graveyard, she and her companions, including her brother Ekaksh, apprentice sorcerer Shloka, dark sorcerers Arit and Asmi, and young Viansh, battle dark forces. AzaGka's father, Ashvath, guides her from the spirit world, as she navigates her haunted past, mysterious visions, and supernatural threats.

Amidst recurring nightmares of a tiger, AzaGka encounters an ominous message, *"You are cursed"*, and a series of eerie events that hint at her forgotten past. A Planchette session connects her with the spirit of Tiksha, a powerful figure linked to her childhood. Through fragmented memories, she recalls a traumatic night when a *man-eater* took her mother, fueling her unresolved fears.

Determined to break the cycle, AzaGka hunts the beast terrorizing *Shikaar Nagar*, uncovering demonic forces tied to her past. In a climactic moment, she embraces her hidden power—transforming into a tiger herself—finally confronting and devouring the man-eater. But the battle has only begun, and deeper mysteries of the four worlds still lurk in the shadows…

"Dark is the blood oozing out of a wound, that is decaying, as people around you are panicking, but doing nothing, as you start hallucinating death".

THE SOUND OF DRIPPING BLOOD

Shloka's mind wrenched itself awake, her consciousness clawing its way out of a suffocating abyss. The air was thick, stale, cloaked in a silence so unnatural it made her ears ring. Then, the chanting began. Whispered prayers, low and rhythmic, encircled her like unseen hands, caressing her skin with an icy touch.

Her parents, their voices. Murmuring ancient verses, too close, yet nowhere in sight.

She tried to move. Nothing. Tried to speak. No sound. Her body—paralyzed, trapped inside itself. A scream swelled in her throat, but only silence came forth.

A breath of laughter slithered through the void.

"Don't bother. I've tried everything. There's no way out, until AzaGka finds us", a voice, Arit's voice, chuckled somewhere in the darkness. *"Maybe we're hiding in someone's brain."*

A cold shiver raced down Shloka's spine. Arit? Here? But he wasn't, *"Hold on... who just spoke?"* Abhaya's voice sliced through the blackness, sharp with panic. *"Arit isn't even with us."*

A suffocating stillness followed.

"Arit... can you hear us?" Abhaya whispered, the words barely leaving her lips, as though afraid of being heard by something else. *"Maybe... maybe he's trying to communicate from another world."*

A wet sound. A drip. Another.

Then, a thick, warm drop splattered against Shloka's cheek. Another against her forehead.

Asmi, still sobbing uncontrollably, let out a strangled whimper.

A sickly metallic scent coiled through the air.

Abhaya swallowed hard. Her voice, now a whisper of dread. *"Is that... blood?"*

FADING FOOTSTEPS

> *"I am sleeping*
> *I am eating*
> *I am hunting*
> *I am crying*
> *eating again*
> *I have started*
> *crying again*
> *Everyone is talking*
> *but I am not listening…"*

The first time I transformed, I hated it. The sensation of my body shifting, the weight of something unnatural settling into my bones. It felt like losing myself, piece by piece. But then, I saw something change. I wasn't afraid anymore. I was becoming fearless. Strong. Or maybe, just… Numb.

At first, I tried to keep this darkness hidden, fearing what it meant. But then, I realized darkness isn't something you escape from. It finds you, whether you want it to or not.

And now, here I am, swallowed by it.
"Eyes can't rest,
closing shut at best,
seems like a test,
were even insects
are winning…
From sunrise to sunset,
crawling out of the nest,
in an aimless pursuit,
what needs to be around,
isn't around."

The curse had been on for two weeks now. But I had been too distracted, too caught up helping Ekaksh unravel the mystery of a headless man possessing the elders of Shikaar Nagar, forcing them to hunt mothers of newborns.

Meanwhile, Ram and Daksh had grown restless. Their visions kept pulling them back to the realm they swore to leave behind. And the reason? Their daughter had strayed too far from the path she was supposed to walk.

I had…

Because the curse had already taken Abhaya, Asmi, and Shloka, they had turned into three crows in our backyard, their human lives stolen away. And yet, amidst all this horror, something else happened, something I never imagined was possible.

I got my father back.

For the first time ever, I was with him. Ashvath. The man whose love I had spent my whole life craving, whose absence had left a wound inside me that never truly healed. Now, he was here, in my world, and it felt like childhood again.

We spent hours in the in-house library, sipping tea, lost in conversations that I had always wished we could have had. I waited for him to return from his college, just like I used to. We went on long evening walks, stopped at the ice cream stall like we had done when I was little.

It was everything I had ever wanted. But it wasn't real.

Deep down, I knew.

Ram's voice shattered the illusion like a blade tearing through flesh, *"Are you not going to break the curse, AzaGka?"* His voice was sharp, cutting through the air as he barged into my room.

I barely acknowledged him, lost in the song playing on my gramophone, Mukesh's haunting voice echoing through the dimly lit space – *"Yeh Mera Deewanapan Hai..."*

"Of course, I'm looking out for them", I said, my voice lighter than I felt. *"What makes you think I'm not?"*

"What you're seeing is a distraction", Ram warned. *"It's meant to keep you trapped."*

His words hit like a fist to the gut, but I refused to let them settle.

"He's never going to come back", he added, softer this time, but with more weight than before.

I stood up abruptly, the warmth in my chest turning to ice.

"Enough", I muttered, brushing past him, my footsteps echoing in the corridor.

I couldn't listen anymore. I didn't want to.

Instead, I went looking for Ekaksh, Viansh, and Arit. It was time to start dinner. Time to focus on anything but the truth clawing in my mind.

That if I chose to break the curse… I would lose my father all over again.

03

THE SOUND OF ECHOES

Present Day – Shikaar Nagar

AzaGka stood by the broken railway tracks, the wind whispering something only she could hear. The cold metal beneath her fingertips sent a shiver down her spine. It had been two weeks since the curse took Abhaya, Asmi, and Shloka, turning them into crows - watching her from the old peepal tree in their backyard.

Two weeks since she had got back something she had longed for her entire life, her father, Ashvath.

But Ram was right. This wasn't real. It was the curse's way of making her forget what she needed to do. And yet, how could she willingly destroy the only time she'd ever get with her father?

The fog thickened around her. The tracks stretched into the void like an open mouth waiting to swallow her whole.

Somewhere behind her, the sound of a train whistle echoed - long, haunting, even though no train was scheduled to pass.

That's when the memories started pulling her under.

Flashback – The Vanishing Man

Ashvath's father had always said that the railway tracks held secrets. They carried echoes of the dead, stories that were never spoken aloud.

That night in December, the fog was thicker than usual. The train had come to a sudden halt at the wrong station. It wasn't supposed to stop there. But power failures were frequent, and his duty as an electrical engineer for the Indian Railways meant working odd hours, fixing unexpected breakdowns.

As he walked with his two assistants toward the central control system, the flickering oil lamp barely cut through the mist. And then, he saw him.

A lone figure, walking away.

Ashvath's father called out, warning him that the train was standing on the opposite track. But the man didn't turn back. Didn't even hesitate.

A train came roaring through the station. The impact should have been immediate flesh against steel, the undeniable finality of life meeting death. But when he and his staff rushed to the spot, expecting a mangled body…

There was nothing.

No blood. No remains. Just an eerie silence that stretched beyond the tracks.

It wasn't the first time he had seen someone disappear into thin air. It wouldn't be the last.

Present Day – AzaGka's Dilemma

AzaGka felt her pulse quicken. The stories were merging, past and present twisting together like two hands gripping her throat.

She thought of Ashvath's childhood, how he grew up watching his father chase ghosts on railway lines. How his mother lost her mind when Avannya was taken by the thing in the forest. How she abandoned him to live in isolation, trying to find something that could never be brought back.

And now, here she was, on the same path—chasing ghosts, clinging to something already gone.

Behind her, a voice whispered., *"AzaGka, come inside. You shouldn't be here."*

She turned. Ashvath stood in the mist, just as she remembered him - tall, handsome, the kind of father she always wished she had more time with.

But she could feel it now. The weight of unreality in his presence. The cold truth pressing down on her chest.

Ram's voice from earlier echoed in her mind: *"He's never coming back."*

A sharp pain surged through her skull. The curse was feeding on her weakness. The longer she stayed here, the harder it would be to let go.

Somewhere in the distance, three crows screeched. Her sisters. Still waiting.

Ashvath smiled. *"Let's go home, beta."*

AzaGka's hands trembled. If she chose to stay, she would lose them forever. If she broke the curse, she would have to lose her father again.

The sound of an approaching train filled the air, drowning out her thoughts. She had to decide. Before the past swallowed her whole.

04

THE HEADLESS MAN

Present Day – Shikaar Nagar

The trees whispered warnings. Blood dripped from the leaves. A foul stench lingered in the air, rotting flesh mixed with wet earth.

AzaGka and Ekaksh crouched behind an overgrown banyan tree, their breaths slow, measured.

"They're close", Ekaksh muttered. *"I can feel it."*

AzaGka's golden eyes gleamed in the dim moonlight, her muscles tense. She could sense the darkness slithering through the air, something old, something rotten.

Ahead, three elder men knelt before an altar, their blank, soulless eyes reflecting the flickering flames. The newborn was still alive. The witch stood in front of them, her robes drenched in blood.

"Do you recognize her?" Ekaksh whispered.

AzaGka's heart pounded. The figure was hooded, face obscured. Something about her felt familiar, yet completely foreign.

Then, from behind them, a woman's voice trembled in the night.

"You won't see her face", she whispered. *"No one does. But I know what she does. I've seen what she leaves behind."*

AzaGka turned sharply.

The woman was thin, gaunt, her saree torn at the edges. Dark circles carved into her face, and her hands trembled as she clutched her shawl.

"Who are you?" Ekaksh asked, stepping closer.

She swallowed hard. *"My name is Leela. And my husband... my husband is one of them."*

Flashback – Leela's Nightmare

Two weeks ago, Leela had been just another housewife in Shikaar-Nagar.

Her husband, Sadhan, was a quiet man. He had been sick for months, barely able to leave his bed. His body was weak. His voice was weak.

Until the night she saw the shadow.

It started by the window. At first, it was just a shape, tall and featureless, watching her through the glass. She thought it was a thief, but thieves don't hover.

She rushed outside, calling for the servants. But when she reached the backyard, she saw something worse - A man with no head.

His shadow stretched across the dirt, reaching her trembling feet.

She choked on a scream as it climbed the wall and vanished.

Heart pounding, she ran inside, only to find her husband sitting up.

He was never awake at that hour.

"Sadhan?" she whispered.

He turned his head, his voice low, guttural. *"I'm hungry."*

The way he spoke, it wasn't him. His tongue curled unnaturally, the words rolling in a language she didn't understand.

Something was inside him. She sent for a "Faqir" *(a religious man who can spiritually detect and cure evil possession).*

When the old man arrived, he took one look at Sadhan and murmured a single word: *"Possessed."*

Present Day – The Ritual in the Woods

AzaGka's jaw tightened as she listened to Leela's story.

"So, you're saying your husband, he's one of them now," Leela whispered. *"He left the house three days ago. I saw him... following the headless man into the woods. I know he's here."*

Ekaksh's eyes darkened. *"If he's with the others, we can still save him."*

AzaGka exhaled. *"But we need him alive. We need to know how this started."*

Ahead, the witch raised her hands, her chant growing louder. The headless man twitched violently.

The elders convulsed, their mouths moving as if whispering secrets only the dead could understand.

Leela clutched AzaGka's arm. *"Please. Get him back."*

AzaGka met Ekaksh's gaze. *"We are moving now."*

The Battle

They struck like shadows in the night.

Ekaksh grabbed one of the elders, knocking him unconscious before he could react.

AzaGka lunged toward the newborn, slashing at the ropes binding its tiny limbs.

The witch turned.

A voice, low, cruel, ancient, spilled from beneath her hood, *"Too late, my children."*

The elder men began screaming.

Before AzaGka could react, their bodies burst apart, torn by invisible claws. Their blood sprayed across the altar, their bones snapping like dry twigs.

The witch laughed.

"You can't save the dead." she whispered.

AzaGka roared. Her body shuddered, bones shifting, muscles stretching, and then, where she once stood, a massive white tiger emerged. Fur as pale as death, eyes burning gold, claws like knives.

The headless man twitched violently, stepping backward.

AzaGka pounced.

Her claws ripped into his chest, sending him crashing to the ground. His body convulsed, dark smoke pouring from his open wound.

He wasn't human anymore. He was something cursed.

Ekaksh, meanwhile, had already found Sadhan. He pressed a sacred talisman onto his chest, and the possessed man howled, his body jerking violently as the darkness inside him writhed, unwilling to let go.

The witch screamed from the altar, her voice inhuman, filled with rage.

AzaGka turned to her, teeth bared, blood dripping from her fangs.

The witch stepped back. *"You think you've won?"*, she hissed.

And then—

She vanished into the mist.

The Aftermath

The forest fell silent.

AzaGka transformed back, panting, her hands still stained with blood.

Leela ran to Sadhan, shaking him. *"Sadhan! Sadhan, wake up!"*

His eyes fluttered open.

AzaGka knelt beside him. *"You're free now. But you need to talk."*

Sadhan coughed, his face still pale from the possession. He looked at AzaGka—and shuddered.

"You don't understand", he whispered. *"You can't stop her."*

Ekaksh frowned. *"Who is she?"*

Sadhan's fingers dug into the dirt.

"The witch. She is... older than this land. Older than the trees. She..". He choked on the words.

AzaGka narrowed her eyes. *"What?"*

His gaze met hers.

"She's been waiting", he murmured. *"For you."*

The trees shuddered. And somewhere in the shadows, the witch laughed.

05

THE TREE OF DEATH

Present Day – Sadhan's Warning

Sadhan's body trembled. *"The witch… she knows you're coming."*

AzaGka narrowed her eyes. *"Then she should be afraid."*

Ekaksh placed a hand on her shoulder. *"No, AzaGka. You don't understand. She's not alone."*

The wind howled through the trees. The shadows moved.

And then, a voice. Low. Raspy. Not human - *"She has called the **Death Mother.**"*

AzaGka's heart stopped.

Death Mother. She knew the name. She had heard the stories.

A woman who once belonged to the living but now ruled the night creatures and the dead.

A woman who could tear open the gates of the afterlife and pull the souls of death eaters into the world of the living.

A woman who had vanished into the forest decades ago.

A woman who was her grandmother.

Flashback – The Birth of a Monster

Shikaar Nagar, years ago. The night Avannya was taken, Ashvath's mother did not cry.

She did not beg.

She did not return home.

She walked into the dark forest, barefoot, her heart black with grief.

The witch's laughter followed her through the trees.

"Your daughter is mine", the voice hissed from the shadows.

Ashvath's mother did not stop walking. She went deeper. The forest welcomed her.

It whispered to her. Called her.

She walked until her body ached. She walked until her feet bled. She walked until she collapsed beneath the branches of a dying tree - The Tree of Death.

And that night—she died.

But she did not stay dead. The forest brought her back. Her body twisted, reshaped, reawakened. Her bones cracked. Her teeth sharpened. Her hands became claws. She rose from the ground, no longer human. Her skin was cold, her heart hollow.

And when she looked into the river, she did not see her face. She saw the golden eyes of a beast.

A werewolf. A creature of the night.

But she was more than that. The vultures circled her. The bats flew at her command. The owls whispered secrets of the dead into her ears. And when she raised her hands to the sky, the gates of the afterlife trembled. She could summon the death eaters, the spirits of those who had been trapped between the worlds - Hungry. Restless. Waiting to be unleashed.

And so, she became their mother - The Death Mother. *A Curse in the Blood*

The witch came to her one final time, *"You have become a monster, just like me."* But Ashvath's mother did not answer. She only waited. waited for the right moment. The right time. To tear the witch apart. To devour her soul. To end her.

But the witch was clever. She knew the Death Mother could not be tamed, so she cursed her bloodline - A curse that would bind all her descendants to the world of the dead. A curse that would force her own grandchildren into her grasp. A curse that would steal Ashvath's life.

And when Ashvath died in an accident years later, he too—was reborn. With the curse of the wolf.

Present Day – The Hunt Begins

AzaGka's breath came fast.

Her father had died, but he had not stayed dead. The same curse that had created the Death Mother had transformed him.

And now—it was coming for her.

The forest whispered to her. The wind carried the laughter of the witch. And far away, in the black abyss of the night, the Death Mother was watching.

Waiting. For her granddaughter to join her. For the curse to claim another soul.

AzaGka clenched her fists.

"Not today."

Her golden eyes flashed. The tiger inside her growled in fury. She wasn't afraid of the dark. She wasn't afraid of the dead. And she wasn't afraid of her grandmother.

The hunt had begun.

06

THE PORTAL OF ENDLESS NIGHT

Prologue: The Fracture of Time and Space

In the dead of night, reality itself seemed to tremble and unravel—threads of time and space interweaving into a tapestry of unspeakable horror. The world was no longer confined to the linear progression of moments but stretched into dimensions where past, present, future, and the realms beyond merged into one relentless nightmare.

Part One: The Cursed Siblings

In a decrepit, abandoned house on the outskirts of a forgotten town, three siblings - Shloka, Asmi, and Abhaya - were ensnared by a curse that twisted their very souls. Under the command of a tattered, hooded witch, they were forced to trudge through shadowed corridors, their hearts pounding in terror. The witch's cruel, hypnotic voice led them to a dilapidated room, where an ancient closet lay ajar, exuding a damp, fetid air.

"This is the threshold", the witch hissed, her tone laced with malice. *"Inside, a monster awaits—its claws, elongated and*

bloodstained, reach for the souls of the innocent. Step forth and serve the realm of death."

In that room, the closet was more than wood and rust; it was a portal, a gateway to a dark realm where lost children were condemned to serve an otherworldly power, their stolen souls fueling an eternal, malevolent energy.

Part Two: The Scooter Ride from Shikaar-Nagar

Miles away, under a leaden November sky, Arit and Viansh were concluding their shift at the Industrial Plant. Exhausted from a long day amid roaring furnaces and clanging metal, they hopped onto their battered Bajaj Chetak. The deserted road home, winding through Indira Gandhi Park and onto a neglected street, was cloaked in a dense, shifting fog.

As they navigated the silent, ghostly thoroughfare, an unsettling sensation crept over them. A weight, almost imperceptible, pressed against the backseat, accompanied by the faint jingle of bangles. From the periphery of their vision, they caught sight of small, delicate feet, an echo of a murdered girl whose spirit had long haunted these very roads. Whispers in the fog told of her restless soul, slipping into vehicles to seek vengeance or solace, an omen of the dark forces at work.

The scooter's headlights cut through the murk, and in that fleeting beam of light, the boundary between worlds blurred. The road twisted and contorted into a spectral corridor, a portal into the dark realm where death reigned and the echoes of tortured souls permeated the air.

Part Three: Convergence in the Dark Realm

Before they knew it, the scooter ride led Arit and Viansh to a shocking destination: the very abandoned house where the cursed siblings now languished. In a moment that defied time, the familiar asphalt and fog melted away into a realm where past, present, and unearthly dimensions collided.

In this four-dimensional space, visions overlapped. Arit and Viansh saw multiple reflections of the world around them: the tortured faces of Shloka, Asmi, and Abhaya being coerced toward the ominous closet, the spectral image of the murdered girl drifting past like a silent warning, and the looming figure of the witch orchestrating the macabre ritual.

Every step inside the house sent shivers through their very souls. The walls pulsated with an eerie energy, as if the building itself was a living, breathing entity, its crumbling facade a canvas for nightmares. In a disorienting interplay of dimensions, the abandoned hallways revealed fleeting glimpses of other times. A child's laughter echoing in a long-forgotten memory, the distant cry of despair from the cursed siblings, and the ragged whispers of the dead melding into a single, chilling cacophony.

Driven by equal parts dread and determination, Arit and Viansh dismounted their scooter and approached the house. The spectral door they had unwittingly crossed through now beckoned them deeper into the labyrinth of horrors. In one mirrored reflection, they witnessed the witch commanding the siblings to step into the closet, each step sealing their fate. In another, the haunted visage of the murdered girl floated by, a silent harbinger of the darkness to come.

Part Four: The Four-Dimensional Descent

In the heart of this interdimensional nightmare, the boundaries between life and death, time and space, unraveled. The cursed siblings trembled as the witch's voice echoed, a sound that resonated in multiple dimensions at once:

"Step forth into the abyss and embrace the power of death!"

At that moment, the closet door creaked open further, revealing a hidden chamber where a monstrous presence lurked. Long, serrated claws scraped the wood, and from the darkness emerged the silhouette of a creature born of nightmares, a being that snatched the souls of children to fuel its unholy dominion. Its eyes glimmered with a hunger that transcended mortal comprehension.

Simultaneously, Arit and Viansh found themselves standing at the threshold of a swirling vortex, a spectral door that connected their world to the realm of the dead. The scooter's engine, now a distant memory, was replaced by the beating of their own hearts and the sound of time splintering. The air grew icy, and the screams of lost souls filled the void, urging them to confront the unyielding darkness.

In this four-dimensional moment, every dimension converged. The tortured cries of Shloka, Asmi, and Abhaya merged with the eerie silence of the abandoned house. The ghostly presence from the scooter ride, the spectral murdered girl, interwove with the sinister power of the closet monster. Arit and Viansh, caught between the remnants of a mortal world and the clutches of an otherworldly realm, knew that their fate was inextricably bound to the curse that had claimed so many.

As they steeled themselves to step through the spectral door, their eyes reflected a determination born of desperation and courage. The dark realm beckoned with promises of answers and the risk of eternal damnation. In that moment, the four dimensions of reality fused into a single, harrowing point of no return.

Epilogue: The Unending Night

In the endless night that followed, the boundaries between worlds remained shattered. The curse of the abandoned house, the spectral scooter ride from Rourkela, and the interdimensional descent of souls intertwined into a tapestry of horror. The witch's cruel laughter, the tormented cries of the siblings, and the relentless echoes of the dead formed a chorus that promised this was only the beginning, a prelude to a horror that would seep into every dimension of existence.

Arit and Viansh now stood at the edge of the abyss, ready to confront the darkness that lay beyond, knowing that the journey into the dark realm would forever change the nature of their reality.

07

BEYOND THE WALLS OF THE GRAVE KEEPER

In the twilight between dimensions, AzaGka stood before a spectral barrier known only as the Walls of the Grave-keeper, a living mosaic of her father Ashvath's childhood memories and the dark legends of "Aghori Baba" *(Grave keepers)*. The wall shimmered with overlapping realities: ghostly faces from the past, swirling mists of forgotten graves, and flashes of lightning that recalled the eerie night Ashvath once raced along Khan Nagar's cemetery.

Crossing the Threshold

Drawing deep from the reservoir of her lineage, AzaGka closed her eyes and leapt into her father's memories. In one breath, she was Ashvath. A wide-eyed teenager pedaling home under a moonless "Krishna Paksha" night *(moonless night)*. He had taken a shortcut alongside the ancient cemetery, where a towering, shadowed figure with braided hair, an Aghori, sat silently on the crumbling wall, a guardian of the dead. That vision, etched into his memory, now served as her key.

As AzaGka opened her eyes in this interdimensional moment, the walls around her parted like the curtains of a haunted theater. She stepped through and into the realm of the death eaters, a world where time, memory, and dark magic converged. Here, spectral voices whispered the truth of a tragic Durga Puja carnival: a night of celebration turned into a nightmare, when a monstrous accident claimed the lives of her mother and many others.

The Shattered Carnival of Memories

In this fractured space, AzaGka met the luminous apparition of her grandmother, a keeper of long-hidden truths. With sorrowful eyes, her grandmother recounted the real tale: amid the revelry, chaos erupted as a malevolent force, later known only as the Soul-sucker, descended upon them. Ashvath, in a desperate bid to save her mother, had transformed into a mighty wolf. In that fierce, primal moment, he fought against the encroaching darkness, even as horrid rumors spread that he had slain his own wife. Yet the true horror lay in the Soul-sucker, its identity and its lingering presence remained shrouded in mystery. Was it a being of pure malice, still stalking the living, hidden among them?

Rescue in the Abandoned House

Back in a parallel fragment of this four-dimensional tapestry, Arit and Viansh battled for life in an abandoned house where terror had taken human form. Within a decaying corridor, a closet hid a monster with ragged, elongated nails, a creature intent on devouring the souls of the innocent.

Viansh, calling upon his shapeshifter gifts, morphed into a swift, spectral panther. In fluid motion, he leapt upon the creature, tearing through the dark energy that bound it. Simultaneously, Arit invoked ancient black magic, summoning sigils that flared with forbidden light and held the beast in thrall. Their combined prowess freed Asmi, who had been teetering on the brink of being consumed and paved a frantic escape from the house.

Convergence and the Final Question

Now, the threads of fate have converged. AzaGka, having traversed her father's memories, now stood at the edge of the death eater's domain. Before her, stretched a realm where spectral figures roamed freely, where time was a labyrinth of past regrets and future terrors. Her grandmother's revelations echoed in her heart as she faced the lingering question: Was the Soul-sucker, that enigmatic force blamed for the ruin of her family, still among the living, waiting to reclaim its power?

Meanwhile, the rescued siblings from the abandoned house joined forces with Arit and Viansh, their escape marking a temporary victory in a war that spanned dimensions. With the spectral portal trembling behind her, AzaGka realized that to break the curse and uncover the Soul-sucker's true identity, she must venture deeper into this interwoven realm of memories and dark magic.

In that final moment, as the wall of the Grave-keeper faded into swirling mists, the line between past and future blurred—a promise of answers yet to be unearthed, and a warning that the true horror was only just beginning.

08

THE PROPHECY

In the depths of the interdimensional realm, where the boundaries of life and death blurred into a kaleidoscope of shifting memories, AzaGka advanced cautiously. The spectral corridor pulsed with eerie energy as the death eaters. A congregation of lost souls and forgotten nightmares, drifted in silent formation. Amidst them, a commanding presence emerged from the blackened void.

Draped in a tattered black robe that billowed like midnight smoke, a towering figure appeared. Her visage that of a vulture, its gaunt features carved from sorrow and ancient wisdom. A flock of bats swirled around her in a frenetic dance, their wings beating a staccato rhythm against the oppressive silence. As she drew closer, the figure's form shimmered and shifted. In one fleeting moment, the vulture's silhouette rippled into that of a fierce wolf; in the next, it morphed into the silent, watchful eyes of an owl. With a final, disquieting transformation, the creature settled once more into its original guise, a vulture-like grandmother whose gaze held the weight of countless lost souls.

Her eyes, dark and infinite, locked with AzaGka's, and in a voice that resonated like wind through ancient tombs, she spoke:

"Child of our cursed bloodline, the time has come for you to understand the weight of our legacy. The curse festers in the depths of our family, and with it, a looming death is gathering—a death that seeks not merely to end life, but to claim our very essence."

As she spoke, the swirling death eaters fell into a reverent hush, their forms quivering with each syllable of her warning. The grandmother's gaze pierced through the veil of time as she continued, her tone both sorrowful and resolute.

"Your siblings—Shloka, Asmi, and Abhaya—are trapped in the labyrinth of the dark realm, held captive alongside Viansh and Arit by forces far more insidious than mere mortal curses. You must return to that forsaken place and free them from their torment. For among us lurks an unknown—a presence that feasts upon death itself, seeking to harvest souls and turn our lineage into an endless night."

Her words reverberated through the corridor, the gravity of the warning a tangible pressure upon AzaGka's heart. The grandmother's form shimmered once more, the bats and death eaters swirling around her like a cloak of inevitability. In that singular, four-dimensional moment, AzaGka felt the entire tapestry of her cursed heritage unravel before her eyes: the tragic night of the Durga Puja carnival, the desperate howl of Ashvath as he fought in wolf form, and the dark rumors of a Soul-sucker whose identity remained shrouded in mystery.

With a final, mournful cry that echoed through both time and spirit, her grandmother's vulture-like form extended a skeletal hand.

"Go now, my child", she intoned. *"Return to the realm of living and free your kin. Lift the curse before the unknown that craves death claims what is left of our light."*

As the spectral vision faded into the swirling mists of the realm, AzaGka's resolve crystallized. The path ahead was perilous, the stakes beyond measure. Yet, with the chilling prophecy of her vulture-grandmother etched into her soul, she stepped away from the ethereal threshold, ready to confront the darkness, rescue her siblings, and uncover the true nature of the unknown force that hungered for death.

09

SHADOWS IN THE SILENT HOUSE

Inside the House

Ekaksh, Ram, and Daksh huddled together in the dimly lit living room of the old house. Outside, the wind howled like a restless spirit, and the dark silence was abruptly shattered by a bloodcurdling shriek. Without warning, a spectral figure, the headless man, materialized in the doorway, his ragged cloak swirling like mist around him.

Ram's eyes widened as the headless man lunged forward with unnatural speed. The trio scrambled for cover. Daksh, ever the cautious one, backed into a corner while Ekaksh steeled himself for a fight, though they knew that mortal weapons might prove useless against such a being.

The Haunting of the Hospital

Miles away in a cold, sterile hospital room, Sadhan lay in a battered bed, his eyes darting in restless terror. Recently rescued, he now suffered from nightmares that left him drenched in sweat. In the dead of night, Sadhan's mind returned to his grim past, a time when he worked as a safety officer at the Rourkela Steel Plant.

He recalled that fateful night shift when, desperate to rest, he had unknowingly chosen a recently repainted bed in the first aid department. The bed, unmarked by its new coat of paint, concealed a dark reputation. As he drifted off, he was tormented by vivid visions— a man, bound to the bed by unseen forces, writhing in endless agony. In his nightmare, Sadhan could see the man's paralyzed face, eyes pleading for release as he struggled in a silent torment that Sadhan felt deep in his bones.

Even after awakening with a jolt, Sadhan couldn't shake the terror. The memory of that haunted bed was now intertwined with his present agony, as he feared that the horror he'd experienced might be more than just a bad dream.

A Collision of Nightmares

Back at the house, the headless man's assault intensified. Ekaksh ducked as the ghostly assailant's formless hands reached out, and Ram's shouts of alarm filled the room. They fought desperately to push the specter back, but each moment drew them deeper into a realm of unspeakable dread.

In a fragmented, two-dimensional overlap of time and fate, Sadhan's nightmare echoed in his mind, the inescapable feeling of being trapped, just like the tormented figure on that cursed bed. As the echoes of horror resonated in his hospital room, he could almost see the swirling shadow of the headless man that now haunted the house with his former companions.

The Silent Plea

Inside the house, as the headless man finally receded into the darkness, Ekaksh, Ram, and Daksh gathered themselves in shock. They knew that the attack was not an isolated incident; a deeper, malignant force was at work. In hushed, trembling voices, they recalled similar stories of restless souls and cursed relics, a tapestry of dread that now bound them all.

Simultaneously, Sadhan lay there, tormented by visions of that haunted bed, unable to discern where his nightmare ended, and reality began. His mind screamed silently, a desperate plea for relief from the lingering specters of his past.

The Unspoken Connection

In that chilling moment, the shared horror of both groups became unmistakably clear: the same dark force that haunted Sadhan's nights at the steel plant had reached into the heart of the abandoned house. The headless man's attack was a manifestation of an ancient curse, a curse that connected every tortured soul in this sprawling, bleak night.

As Ekaksh, Ram, and Daksh slowly rose from their hiding place, and the curse that now bound them all. And in the hospital, as Sadhan fought off the terror of his nightmares, he too realized that the horror was far from over. It had only just begun.

In the silent corridors of both the house and the hospital, the shadows whispered of deeper, darker secrets, and the night promised that the true horror was yet to come.

10

SHADOWS IN THE SILENT HOUSE

In the sterile gloom of the hospital, Sadhan's nightmares reached a fevered crescendo. The tormented visions of the cursed bed and unending torment gnawed at his sanity until, with trembling resolve, he rose from his bed. Drawn by an irresistible call, he left the antiseptic corridors behind, stepping into the suffocating embrace of the night.

Outside, the inky darkness whispered his name, guiding him toward a spectral threshold, the very realm that had long held the cursed siblings captive. Each step was heavy with despair and inevitability as Sadhan followed the call into a chasm where time and reality blurred.

In an instant, the oppressive darkness engulfed him. From the swirling shadows, the headless man emerged with feral grace. His ragged form reached out, and with a horrifying swiftness, he seized Sadhan, dragging him into his spectral maw. In that ghastly moment, Ekaksh, already caught in a struggle against forces beyond mortal ken, was wrenched away. His anguished cry melding with Sadhan's as both were swallowed by the abyss.

Back in the crumbling living room, the chaos took its toll. Ram and Daksh lay unconscious on the cold floor, their bodies motionless amid the flickering lights that cast grotesque, dancing shadows across the walls, a silent, eerie witness to the unfolding nightmare.

The house, now a nexus of terror, pulsed with malevolent energy. In that final, shattering instant, the barrier between the living and the dead dissolved entirely, leaving only darkness, despair, and the inescapable grip of the cursed realm.

11

THE ROAD OF LOST MEMORIES

AzaGka plunged back into the dense, brooding forest of Shikaar Nagar, her heart heavy with the weight of her family's shattered fate. She was in search of the abandoned house, a cursed refuge where her siblings were stranded. The forest's silence was broken by distant, anguished shouts. Ram, seething with fury over Daksh's unexplained absence, roamed the dim paths. In his desperation, he called out to Tiksha, his dead wife, imploring her spectral guidance to help find either Ashvath or AzaGka.

At that very moment, Tiksha's form shimmered into existence. Clad in ethereal darkness, she transformed into a fierce, majestic tiger. Her eyes glowed with otherworldly resolve as she prowled beside Ram. From another realm, a heart-wrenching howl tore through the night, a sound both mournful and commanding. It was Ashvath, his spectral wolf form guiding AzaGka with fierce paternal love across the shifting dimensions.

In that poignant instant, AzaGka understood: the only way to traverse into Ashvath's world, the realm of the dead, was to unlock the buried memories of her past.

With trembling determination, she let the memories carry her across the dimensional divide.

Emerging into the world of the dead, guided by her father's ghostly presence, AzaGka found herself before a grim scene. Ram lay wounded, his eyes filled with silent agony, while Tiksha, overcome with sorrow, sat by his side, tears streaming down her face. *"Am I losing Ram?"* she whispered, the question echoing in the stillness of that spectral plane.

Before she could tend to their pain, a new terror awaited her. Recalling her grandmother's dire warnings, AzaGka set off along a desolate, twisting road where the boundaries of reality frayed. In the flickering half-light, she encountered bizarre, nightmarish beings: creatures with the torso of a cow and the head of a howling dog. Their guttural cries and frenzied pursuit sent shockwaves of fear through her. They swarmed like a pack of ravenous beasts, their forms shifting and overlapping in the four-dimensional chaos of the dark realm.

AzaGka fought desperately against the relentless assault. Bruises blossomed across her skin as she dodged and weaved through the onslaught, her mind racing for a way to escape. In a moment of desperate clarity, she leapt into a vivid, searing memory, one from her past that held the key to salvation. The memory unfolded like a portal, and with one final bound, she disappeared from the tormented road, reappearing at the threshold of the abandoned house.

Breathless and battered, she stood before the crumbling edifice, a monument to lost hope and lingering curses. Within those dilapidated walls, her siblings waited in uncertain limbo, and the echoes of her family's tragic past reverberated like a dirge. Now, with Ram grievously wounded and the spectral forces of the dark realm closing in, AzaGka knew that every moment was precious. The curse had to be broken before the unknown, a force that craved death, could claim them all.

Steeling herself, AzaGka prepared to step inside, determined to rescue her kin and confront the shadowy secrets that had haunted her family for generations.

12

THE SHATTERED VEIL

I stepped through the shattered threshold of the abandoned house one last time, each step a descent deeper into the nightmare of my past and our cursed present. In that forsaken place, I became Avannya once more, revisiting the dark memory of a nine-year-old girl, abused and broken by a monster in human guise. The echoes of that torment reverberated in every creaking corridor.

In the gloom of a dungeon far below, headless men labored over a blazing firepit, their crude blades slicing through rotting flesh. Amid the chaos, the witch emerged, her face hidden beneath a tattered veil. As the dim light shifted, her features began to reveal themselves in agonizing fragments. Before I could muster a cry, a searing blow from behind plunged me into darkness.

When I awoke, disjointed visions assaulted me. I found myself in the midst of a spectral battle. My father, Ashvath, once my unwavering guide, even as he howled in his wolf form, was nowhere to be found in any realm now. His protective presence had vanished, swallowed by the darkness that claimed him long ago. My grandmother, that fearsome vulture cloaked in sorrow and ancient power, fought valiantly alongside forces I barely understood, her bat-like minions circling overhead.

Ram, his face a mask of fury and grief, urged me, *"Take your siblings and run!"* But as I gathered the survivors, Asmi, Arit, and Viansh, I realized with a crushing weight that Abhaya was no more. The witch's wrath had torn her from us in a single, horrific moment; the wind had seized her delicate form and ripped her apart before my very eyes.

Desperation surged as I clutched the reins of a battered jeep, our only escape from the clutches of that accursed place. Amid the howling dark, a creature of indescribable horror pursued us, a beast with shifting features, capable of rending flesh as though it were paper. In the distance, my heart seized in terror: Daksh, transformed into the Soul-sucker, held Shloka captive, suspending her lifeless form from a gnarled tree. Shloka, my dearest friend, the one soul I had hoped to save, was lost to that unspeakable void.

In the ensuing chaos, Ekaksh, now a vessel for the headless man's sinister power, appeared in the middle of the road. With terrifying, inhuman strength, he hurled our jeep until it tumbled, scattering us into the abyss of shattered reality. Amid the cacophony of screams and clashing shadows, Ram, his voice raw with anguish, implored, *"Leave now!"* but it was too late.

I ordered Viansh and Arit to scramble up the wall, carrying the wounded Asmi and the broken remnants of Abhaya. Yet, every moment was a countdown to our final undoing. As I turned, the witch reappeared, a specter of malice and regret. With a gust of vengeful wind, she seized Abhaya's memory, her form twisting into a nightmarish mockery of life, and in one merciless blow, erased what was left of her.

In a surge of raw, desperate power, I transformed. I morphed into a fierce amalgam of all my terror and resolve. I charged at the witch, ripping open her veil with a strength born of sorrow and fury. But as the mask fell away, I was met not with the face of a demon, but that of my own mother. A visage filled with regret, pleading silently for forgiveness. Her presence halted my rage, and in that shattering moment, I knew the curse was broken, but at a terrible cost.

The backyard, once ruled by a horde of cawing crows, now lay eerily silent. I sat alone in the dim light of an indifferent morning, eating a cookie, reading a newspaper, as if mocking the horror that had transpired. I had lost Shloka, my only friend, and my father was gone, lost in the realms from which no echo returned. The remnants of my family - Ekaksh, Viansh, Asmi, and Arit - remained, battered and broken, a fragile reminder of what we had survived.

I gazed into the distance, haunted by the promise I once made: to venture back into that abyss, to rescue Shloka from the clutches of the Soul-sucker, and to reclaim what was lost. For now, I carry this burden, a legacy of pain and hope, knowing that though the curse may be broken, the scars of our souls will endure in the endless twilight of memory.

"Feet would float,
Music would stride,
Singing while flying...
In my father's scooter..
That glides...
Standing upright,
Right next to the headlights,
Gripping the lights tighter,
While feeling lighter,
As the twists and turns,
Went out of sight...
Like the arms of a wounded fighter..
Family of four,
In a wheel of three,
A picnic, a restaurant or a department store,
In the marching spree,
While I felt free,
Stalled at my scooter's best seat..
Sneaking a treat,
Or smirking a fleet..
Make way for the horn,
For here comes the feeling
To experience which you were born...
Holding onto a wedding gift,
Or a toy to play,
there was always plenty of room to stay,
Afternoons pretending to ride,
Friends coming over to stand beside,
Catching a nap,

Or hidden behind soothing a bumpy trap,
Always doing what's told,
Striking that bold look,
Aced that sturdy equalizer..
I grew tall
but dad never made the call
for me to take the back seat,
as he knew I loved the streets from the front row,
and couldn't believe that his daughter would one day outgrow...
Waving people,
swerving medieval rush,
was an era that vanished..
as I stood there astonished..
still dusting her out till date,
and keep remembering our first scooter ride..."

"2 MIN HORROR STORIES"
BY JUSTUTTER HORROR

Bonus Stories

**These stories were personal experiences shared by individuals. Any resemblance to anyone else's experiences or life events are purely coincidental.*

Night Study

One night, during our high school days in Brajrajnagar, Odisha, my two friends and I were cramming for our board exams. When we finally finished studying, one friend had to walk several blocks back to his place. He warned us that his neighborhood would become deserted and shrouded in darkness very soon, so he decided to start his journey early.

About half an hour later, I heard him shouting desperately at the entrance gate, pleading for it to be opened. He was drenched in sweat and gasping for breath, and he begged me to accompany him this time.

Based on his account, here's how the terrifying experience unfolded:

"I was walking along the roadside when I reached a particularly dark bend. In the middle of the road, a few cows grazed idly, accompanied by stray dogs meandering about. As I cautiously made my way past them, I suddenly sensed someone's presence watching me from a distance. I could just make out the upper half of a man's body, peeking from behind the backdoor of a nearby house.

The moment I saw him, every animal around me became agitated, the cows shifted uneasily, and the dogs erupted into furious barks as if warning me of imminent danger. I tried to quicken my pace, but to my horror, I noticed that the man's lower body was not human at all, it was that of a snarling dog. Panic surged through me, and without a second thought, I bolted, not daring to look back."

Returning to our own tale, my friend was so terrified that he begged me to accompany him. Overwhelmed by fear, I convinced another friend to join us on the same route. As we walked, we again heard distant, frantic barking, the sound echoing ominously in the night. Determined to avoid the dreadful figure, we quickly diverted to another friend's nearby house and persuaded him to accompany us back.

Thankfully, when he joined us, we did not encounter the grotesque apparition again. We managed to drop off our terrified friend and finally returned to our own homes. That night left us shaken, and we vowed never again to plan night studies.

The memory of that horrifying encounter, of another worldly figure with the upper body of a man and the lower half of a dog, and the sinister chorus of barking that filled the darkness, remains etched in our minds as a chilling reminder that some paths are best avoided when night falls.

The Feast Amidst the Dead

It was well past midnight, and I was still lying awake, the relentless tick of the clock mocking my futile attempts at sleep. At 2:35 AM, a familiar voice called out from the next room. Slipping on my bedside slippers, I followed the sound, expecting the comforting echoes of a memory long cherished.

As I pushed open the door, I found myself stepping into a realm from my childhood, the familiar grounds of my grandfather's ranch. The flower-laden garden outside the back courtyard was bathed in moonlight, with children laughing and playing, their silhouettes blurred as they ran past one another. I hurried inside, barely glancing at their faces, my heart pounding with a mix of nostalgia and an inexplicable dread.

In the dining hall, my grandfather sat calmly ordering more goat curry for his beloved granddaughter – that's me. The room buzzed with the festive hustle and bustle of a family feast, and the aroma of freshly baked bread mingled with the savory scents wafting from the kitchen, where my grandmother was busy preparing her favorite fish curry.

Then, without warning, the lights flickered and died, plunging everything into impenetrable darkness, as if an abrupt power outage had swallowed the warmth and light whole. I groped my way forward in the inky black, my bare feet navigating a tunnel of shadows. Every step was fraught with uncertainty, and I prayed desperately not to stumble into something unspeakable.

A sudden, blood-curdling scream shattered the silence, emanating from a bedroom window. I caught a glimpse of a shadow slipping through the doorway—a dark figure that sent a shiver racing down my spine. In that frozen moment, time itself seemed to pause. The faces around me dissolved into ghostly silhouettes; insects crawled over my skin as if marking me, while ravens cawed in unison and rats scurried in frenzied chaos.

Desperate for answers, I stumbled into a room in search of my aunts, only to be met by a horrifying sight: dozens of crows, their beady eyes glinting as they peered at me, their sharp beaks tearing into what looked disturbingly like decaying flesh. Panic surged through me. I screamed for help, but my calls were swallowed by the oppressive darkness, and no one, no matter how close, seemed to hear me.

I raced to the terrace, where I spotted my cousin, a lanky figure smoking a cigarette with a group of friends. I waved frantically, but as I approached, his features melted away into the shape of an owl, which took off into the night without a backward glance.

My heart was pounding, and my mind was reeling, I fled back downstairs. In a state of sheer terror and disorientation, I collapsed at the dining table. The feast that had moments ago been full of life now appeared to be a macabre gathering.

Around me sat figures that resembled zombies, motionless, expressionless, as if the very essence of life had been drained from them. I found myself mechanically devouring the food served, each bite a futile attempt to anchor myself to sanity, yet the horror of the scene persisted.

Then, amidst the ghastly assembly, I realized with paralyzing dread that these were not simply hallucinations. The dead had come to meet me, an unholy banquet of the departed, gathered in the eerie glow of a feast meant for the living, yet poisoned by the presence of death.

I sat there, frozen by fear and despair, as the macabre dinner unfolded around me. A nightmarish convergence of memories and specters, a feast of the dead that I would never escape from, no matter how hard I tried.

Walls of the Grave Keeper

If you have ever witnessed what lurks among the dead, you will never dare venture out at night again. If you have ever seen the ghastly sight of a corpse being devoured, you will fear death itself. In certain parts of rural and urban Odisha, particularly around Cuttack, there exist grim guardians known as "Aghori Baba", mysterious grave keepers who belong to a cult that serves the death eaters. I recall, as a wide-eyed teenager, hearing whispers of their frequent appearances at places like Khannagar Cemetery, Sati Chaura Graveyard, and Gora Kabar Graveyard.

My friends and I, driven by a mix of youthful curiosity and morbid fascination, once planned an excursion to these haunted sites during our high school days. Yet, our daytime visits yielded nothing but empty, silent graveyards, devoid of the macabre rituals and gory displays of cannibalism we had been told about, or the dreadful sight of rotting human bones fashioned into grotesque adornments.

One fateful evening, after a long study session at a friend's place, I set out on my bicycle under a moonless sky, the air heavy with the promise of impending rain. In our local folklore, this time of night is known as "Krishna Paksha," when the moon's light is swallowed by darkness. I took a shortcut that cut through the graveyard at Khan Nagar - a path notorious for its oppressive gloom. The road, adjacent to the burial ground, was so dark that I could barely see my own hand before my eyes. The silence was absolute, broken only by the distant, mournful howls of stray dogs.

As I pedaled cautiously, a sudden flash of lightning split the sky, briefly illuminating the macabre scene. In that brief, stark light, I saw a towering black figure seated atop the ancient wall of the graveyard. The figure, draped in darkness with long, tangled locks of braided hair, stared unblinkingly toward the heart of the cemetery. It was as if the very embodiment of death had come to life, silently devouring the darkness around it.

My blood ran cold. I didn't dare linger; I bolted down the street, my heart pounding in terror, desperate to escape the malevolent presence. That night, I left with a haunting conviction: there exists a cult of Aghori Baba—those who walk amidst the dead, feasting on the darkness, and fearless in the face of all that is forbidden.

Hospital Bed

Working as a safety officer in a steel plant is no fun—especially when you're forced to sleep in the first aid department, where victims of horrific accidents are brought in and declared dead. That night, during my night shift, I joined the other staff members near the first aid area. Late at night, we usually dragged ourselves to the beds in that department to stretch our legs and try to catch a few moments of sleep.

One colleague had warned me about a particular bed, a bed said to be cursed, where anyone who slept on it would be haunted by unspeakable horrors. We always avoided that bed at all costs. Unfortunately, earlier that day, the staff had repainted all the beds, making it impossible to tell the cursed one apart from the others. Unwittingly, I chose that very bed to rest on as our shift was nearing its end.

At first, I felt only a slight discomfort as I drifted off. But as the night wore on, grotesque visions invaded my mind. I began to sweat profusely as I saw in vivid detail a hideous figure, a man, his skin mottled and decaying, strangled by invisible forces, his eyes wide with torment, his body contorted in agony as if he were being forced to relive the horrors of his final moments over and over again. The sickening sound of his muffled screams echoed in my ears, and I felt his despair seeping into my very soul.

I tried to shake the bed violently, desperate to break free from the nightmare, but it was as if I were pinned down by an unseen force. My voice caught in my throat when I attempted to scream out to my colleagues, and no sound emerging, only a strangled, silent cry of terror.

Finally, with a forceful, bone-jarring thud, I bolted upright as I tumbled off the bed. I awoke in a cold sweat, heart pounding, the horrors of the nightmare still vivid in my mind. It felt so real that I could almost feel the anguish of the poor soul who had suffered on that cursed bed. A soul that had, in the end, given up and ended his own life.

I couldn't sleep for days after that night, and I warned all my colleagues about that dreadful bed. We eventually had it discarded, but the memory of that night, with its bloodcurdling images and suffocating terror, continues to haunt me.

Night Duty

I was returning from a long, grueling day at the Rourkela Steel Plant. Plant shifts demand unwavering commitment, morning, afternoon, or night. That day I was finishing my afternoon shift, already running late due to a last-minute accident in the blast furnace department that forced me to write a lengthy safety report.

My route from the plant to the company quarters took me through Indira Gandhi Park, where I was forced to take a left onto a deserted street leading to the park maintenance quarters. It was around 11:30 PM, and the area was eerily abandoned, with not a single pedestrian or vehicle in sight. Despite the dense November fog that cloaked the road in ghostly white, the lack of traffic usually made me feel somewhat secure.

Then, as I navigated a bump on my Bajaj Chetak scooter, I suddenly sensed an unusual weight pressing against the back of my seat. Accompanying this strange sensation was the chilling clatter of bangles, a sound that echoed like a death knell in the silent night. Alone on the road, my heart hammered against my chest. I hesitated to stop and investigate, gripped by a mounting sense of dread.

Out of the corner of my eye, I caught a glimpse of something even more horrifying: a pair of delicate feet, likely those of a girl wearing worn-out sandals. In that instant, a ghastly image flashed before me: the pale, bloodless face of a young girl, her eyes vacant and filled with unspeakable sorrow.

Panic surged through me, and without a moment's thought, I accelerated away, leaving the spectral figure behind.

The following day, I learned that a girl had been brutally murdered at that very spot several months earlier. Reports detailed that her body had been savagely torn apart in a manner so gruesome it defied belief. Since that night, disturbing rumors spread among locals: travelers passing through the area at night claimed that her vengeful spirit now haunted their vehicles, her mournful wails and the sinister jingle of her bangles a constant reminder of the horror that lingers in the darkness.

In the Closet

We craved this vacation for a long time. So, three of my friends and family took this well discounted 4-BHK villa, for 2 nights. It was a lovely view from up there, it opened to the lake and spacious sitting arrangements in the front courtyard to have bonfire, merrymaking and outdoor activities. Every one of us did a lot of research on the outdoors, but none of them really paid that much attention to the indoors, as we thought we would spend most of our time outdoors.

Once the trip began, we were excited, all of us had 2 kids each so they were about to keep each other company. On the first night, while I was sleeping, I heard some noise from the closet right next to the bedroom near our room, that wasn't occupied by anyone. I thought of walking in and checking, but instead nervously bolted the door from outside.

The second day, one of the kids got locked in that room while playing hide and seek. The mom panicked, so I rushed to my bedroom, right next to it and opened the connected door back again. The kid came closer and whispered into my ears, that there was someone hidden in the closet, with big nails. I thought she was kidding and ignored her. That night I again heard noises. I couldn't resist and took the torch and stepped in. The room had no lights working, which was strange, but had some light coming from our bedroom. Most of the crowd was outside playing games and drinking, and the kids were asleep in the rooms downstairs. I snuck in and found that there was a walking closet, right adjacent to the window. I noticed someone standing outside the window. As I went closer, the closet opened on its own and I could hardly see anything in the dark but could feel someone breathing from the corner.

I raised my torch and saw a hidden cabinet. At that moment, someone called my name from outside, so I made up my mind to leave, but as I started walking out, I could see a single hand that seemed to be dark and hairy with sharp nails, seeking its way out from that hidden room. I couldn't help but bolt the door from outside rushing out and asked everyone to pack their bags and head back right away. Whatever it was, it was not going to spare any of us, had it found us, especially the kids.

Midnight Lamp

I was an electrical engineer serving the Indian Railways. So usually, I had shifts at odd hours to check electrical controls in railway lines, inside trains, within stations, freight hubs etc., especially during breakdowns and power outages. One such night I was called post-midnight to check on an abrupt shutdown of a train at the wrong station.

It was around the month of December, I was posted in Kharagpur, West Bengal. The tracks were filled with fog, making it real hard to see. I was walking beside my 2-support staff and one of them was holding the oil lamp. As we fixed the issue, rebooting the central control system, the train was back online, the passengers waiting in the station impatiently started to board. While I was heading back to the station control system, to give all okay signal and clearance, I saw a man's shadow at a distance, heading in the opposite direction. As my vision was blurry due to fog and dark night, I started running and shouted at the man saying, the train is standing the other way. But I noticed the man wasn't turning back or paying heed to my voice, he was already at the tail end of the station.

He kept walking and eventually I gave up and started walking back to my office frustrated, as I hated when people used to walk in the railway tracks for shortcuts. Suddenly a train came roaring on that same track and crossed by. I asked my staff to accompany me to check as I was sure to find that man lying dead. But to our surprise we found nothing. Some of my staff members, requested me to head home, as they tried to explain me about an incident that had happened two days back, where a man did commit suicide at the same track. After that I did have a few more incidents, where I used to see weird instances of people disappearing in thin air behind old trains, railway lines, and every time there was a story of a dead person associated with them.

Bonus Story: Beheaded Man

During the winter nights at the Servants of India Society, in Buxi Bazar Cuttack, we used to close our doors quickly in the evening, for the outside used to become dark very early in the evening hours by 6PM. The place was covered with a lot of trees and a dense forest of jackfruit, bananas and guava trees. My husband being in bed all the time, due to his recent health condition, had failed to be up for long at night. He would go to sleep by 8PM and get up by 5AM. There was a tree just next to his bedside window, that would attract a lot of exotic birds that hummed bird songs in the afternoon and morning hours.

One fine evening, I could see an apparition of a man by the window glass, while I was shutting it down. I rushed outside and called out my helpers to see if it was a thief at that time of night. Unfortunately, no one came in, and I had to go alone to the backyard amidst the trees to see who it was. Shockingly I saw a man without a head, walking past the trees, I clearly remember his shadow being quite tall falling right next to my feet that were trembling vigorously at that sight. I looked at it climbing the wall and then vanished in thin air.

I walked back inside to wake up my husband from his afternoon siesta. He was wide awake, and was already calling my name, in a peculiar tone, that wasn't him. He even requested some food, in a language that I didn't even know he was so well versed with. I sensed something wrong and asked my helper to get a "Faqir" *(a religious man who can spiritually detect and cure evil possession)*. I saw a weird looking owl at the tree right next to his window, staring at me as if it was the man himself.

After the Faqir came, he detected an evil spirit inside my husband's body and asked me to make some homemade herbal remedy. He mentioned he is sensing a spirit of a man who was beheaded in the backyard many years ago by the previous landlords, due to which he is visiting the premises till now. He requested me to have my husband wear a "Tabiz" (an amulet), because he was weaker from a health perspective, the spirit will always try to control him. I made sure we cut all the trees close to his window and kept it closed all the time after sunset. He recovered after couple of days, but I still use to see the shadow of the beheaded man for quite some time after that incident, until we left that place for good.

FROM "2 MIN HORROR STORIES" COLLECTION – STORIES FROM READERS

A few more short stories, from my "2 Min Horror Stories" collection shared by "JustUtter" Readers.

Don't forget to visit:

"https://www.justutter.com".

These are personal experiences shared by "JustUtter" Readers.

Let Me Go Home - by a JustUtter Reader as a true experience

It was a dark winter night, and I was returning from Basudebpur to Bhadrak. The day was Diwali so it was moonless night. I was traveling back home in my blue Bajaj Chetak (scooter). The highway was empty, no one was there. I had to travel 40 kilometers to another town, I had to cross 2 rivers, but just before the third river, I had to cross the "Saguan" forests. While crossing the forest, I suddenly saw a woman like figure flying on my left side, her hair covered most of her face.

At first, I thought, I was hallucinating as the forest was very dark and she was really very far away from my sight at first. She was in a white saree; my hand had started to sweat across the handle and feet started to tremble but I prayed to Goddess Durga and kept driving faster. Then I saw her disappear, and thought I was saved and kept chanting my mantras. After a few kilometers, I saw her back again, this time she was heading right towards me from the front. I accelerated my scooter to hit her, but unfortunately my scooter hit an old shop on wheels instead and went completely out of control. I met with a deadly accident and my scooter slides up the road to not sure how many kilometers, I go unconscious. When I opened my eyes, I find myself at a nearby temple, the "Nana" (priest), and the temple staff sprinkling water on my face. The deity from the Dhakineswara Kali temple saved me. I avoided that route for good.

*This incident was shared by a reader claiming this to be a true experience. Any resemblance with any real places or occurrences is still purely fictional and up to the audience's belief.

8 km Stretch: Haunting Encounter - by Tharun Bandarupalle

It was Friday, 11th October 2022, around 2:30 AM in the capital city of Telangana, Hyderabad. I encountered the most horrific and tragic experience of my life while returning home from a party in Gachibowli. It was a windy night, and everything seemed normal until I reached Begumpet.

The area, about 8 km from the Begumpet flyover, is usually bustling with vehicles honking and people enjoying late-night food. That 8 km stretch is famous for its night-time activity. But on this particular night, the silence around me felt strange and unsettling. There was no movement of vehicles, the wind had stopped swirling, and the stillness of the trees sent goosebumps down my spine. I knew something was wrong and realized I needed to be very careful.

Despite the familiar route, I was both uneasy and intrigued, sensing a life-changing experience ahead. Just before entering the 8 km stretch, I paused briefly. To calm my nerves and gather courage, I recited the Hanuman Chalisa.

A few minutes later, I started driving along the stretch. For the first three kilometers, everything seemed normal. There were no signs of anything unusual or paranormal, and I began to feel a sense of relief. But as I reached the fourth kilometer, I saw a diversion sign. It indicated a left turn, forcing me onto a longer route than the one I had planned.

Instead of taking a left, I drove straight through the latter half of the stretch. Once I passed the diversion sign, I started hearing unsettling sounds, like a woman weeping and a child playing. I still remember a woman whispering my name in my ear. Initially, I ignored it and kept going. But the voice grew louder, compelling me to stop and look back. The moment I turned, I saw the shadow of a mysterious girl sitting on the bark of a tree, chanting my name in a firm voice. The image is unforgettable; her face was pale, with dark red eyes that seemed to be made of blood.

I ignored it, terrified, as this was the first of many paranormal activities that night. I tried to continue driving my vehicle, still trying to make sense of what I had just witnessed. A few minutes later, I realized my vehicle was no longer under my control as the speed increased exponentially. I felt as though someone was riding my bike. Despite multiple attempts to regain control, I failed miserably. A few moments later, my vehicle stopped at the sixth kilometer of that stretch.

The moment the vehicle stopped; I saw a shadow materialize right in front of my eyes. I fainted the next second because it was too terrifying. A few minutes later, I heard the same voice screaming my name. I tried to get up and escape from that stretch, but unfortunately, I was lying there, helpless, at the mercy of the witch. I recited the Hanuman Chalisa continuously, without stopping for a second. Then I gathered enough strength to rise and walk toward my vehicle. As soon as I started it, I felt my leg burn as it made contact with the silencer, an invisible force pulling me toward it. I kept reciting the Hanuman Chalisa until I finally reached the end of the eight-kilometer stretch.

The moment I left the area; I saw that my leg was bleeding. Fortunately, an officer came to help me. He took me to a nearby home, where I received initial treatment. The old man who treated me seemed to know exactly what had caused the injury. He took my contact number and asked me to call the next morning. I finally reached home around 6 AM. The next day, around 2:00 PM, I called the old man. He explained in detail what had happened to me the previous night.

I was amazed at how he knew about everything. Then he told me the reason for the eerie silence over the past week. A week earlier, a group of bikers had murdered a woman who was a witch. She now sought revenge, especially targeting those who traveled on two-wheeled sports bikes. Unfortunately, I had used the same type of vehicle, and he advised me to either get rid of the bike or visit a temple and perform the necessary rituals.

I went to the old man's house and took him to a nearby temple. The priest and the old man had a brief conversation. Then, the priest performed rituals that would save me from the witch's wrath. It was a terrifying experience that will stay with me forever.

बारातियों की चीख़ - by Pramod Verma

6 नवंबर 2008 रात के 2:30 बजे, काली सर्दी की रात और वो खूबसूरत चाँद। मैं अभी अभी अपने इवेंट के काम से फ़्री हो कर घर के लिए जल्दी जल्दी निकला था।ऐसा मेरे साथ महीने में 20 दिन हो ही जाता हैं।मैं दिल्ली से अपने घर साहिबाबाद के लिए निकला, आनंद विहार तक तो मैं आसानी से पहुँच गया, अब मुझें यहाँ से टेम्पो पकड़ कर घर के गली तक जाना था। लेकिन कोई भी टेम्पो उस रात नज़र नहीं आ रहीं थी। मैं पैदल यहाँ से आगे नहीं जा सकता था क्योंकि डरावनी जंगल के रास्ते से हो कर जाना पड़ता और मेरी हालत थकान और नींद से बुरी हो रही थी।

स्टैंड पर बैठें बैठें सोने ही वाला था कि अचानक बस का हॉर्न मेरी कान में बजा जिससे मैं घबरा गया। देखा तो एक बस जो सजी हुई हैं फूलों से, बारातियों का बस हैं ये तो, किसी शादी से वापिस जा रही हैं। बस कन्डेक्टर उतर कर स्टैंड के बग़ल के दुकान से बीड़ी खरीदता हैं। कन्डेक्टर काला सा हड्डी जैसा सूखा सा था। फिर मेरी नज़र बस के अंदर पड़ी, सब हँस रहें थे, आपस मे बातें कर रहे थे, मस्ती कर रहे थे। तभी कन्डेक्टर जाने लगता हैं। जाते जाते कंडेक्टर मुझसे पुछता हैं "कहाँ जाओगे?" मैंने कहा "साहिबाबाद, क्यों उधर से ही जा रहें हो क्या तुम।"

कन्डेक्टर "हा उधर से ही जा रहें हैं, चलना हैं तो चलो, लेकिन बीड़ी का ख़र्चा देना होगा।"

मैंने कहा "हा जरूर।" और मैं लपक कर कन्डेक्टर के साथ आगें बैठ गया, ड्राइवर मेरी तरफ़ धीरे से पलटता हैं और कन्डेक्टर से इसारे में बात करता है और फ़िर बस स्टार्ट करता हैं। जंगल के रास्ते पहुँचते ही बहुत धुंध लग गई, पीछे सभी बाराती हँस रहे हैं, गा रहे हैं, लेकिन कन्डेक्टर और ड्राइवर चुप चाप आगें देखते हुए गाड़ी चला रहे हैं, ना इधर देख रहे हैं ना उधर। मैंने अपना सिगरेट निकाला और कंडेरक्टर से पूछा "सिगरेट लोगें?" कंडेरक्टर ने चुपचाप सिगरेट ले लिया और कहा "यहाँ जलाना नहीं बाद में बाहर पी लेना। "

तभी अचानक पीछे सभी बराती जो गा रहे थे, उनकी गाने की आवाज़ रोने में बदल जाती हैं, इतनी बुरी और दर्दनाक रोने की आवाज़ सुन मैं घबरा गया और पीछे देखा। सब ड्राइवर केबिन के बाहर खड़े हैं, रो रहे हैं और कह रहे हैं "बस रोको, रोको, वो आने ही वाला हैं, रोको, हम सब फिर से मरना नहीं चाहते, रोको...."यह सब देख मेरा दिमाग़ चकरा गया हैं, मुझें कुछ समझ नहीं आ रहा है, वहाँ बैठा अब मैं अपने शरीर को हिला नहीं पा रहा हूँ, ना ही अपना मुँह खोल पा रहा हूँ, की ड्राइवर से कुछ पूछ सकू।ड्राइवर कंडेरक्टर को देखता हूँ, दोनों चुपचाप बिना कुछ सुने आगें देख रहे हैं, दोनों के आंख से ख़ून के आँसू बह रहे थे। मैंने बहुत ताक़त लगाया, इतना कि मेरे दाँत कट-कटाने लगे, बहुत ताक़त लगा कर अपना हाथ उठाया और दरवाजा खोलने की कोशिश की, तभी बस का जोरदार टक्कर ट्रक से हो गया, बहुत बुरा एक्सीडेंट। मेरा पूरा शरीर दर्द से टूट गया और सब चीख़ने लगें। उस चीख़ के साथ मेरे कान से ख़ून निकल गया, मैं बोहोश हो गया। और उसी चीख़ के साथ मैं होश में आया तो ख़ुद को हॉस्पिटल में पाया। सब कह रहे थे मैं सड़क पर पड़ा था, मैंने रात की घटना सबकों बताई, किसी ने विस्वास नहीं किया।

फ़िर मैंने अपने मन की संतुष्टि के लिए पता लगाया, तो पता चला। दुर्घटना हुई थी 6 नवंबर 2006 को, दूसरे तरफ़ ट्रक के ड्राइवर ने शराब पी थी, इस वज़ह से धुंध में एक्सीडेंट हुआ था। बस में सिर्फ 4 लोग बचे थे, बाक़ी सब मर गए थे।

इसके बाद वो बस हर साल, 6 नवंबर को किसी न किसी को दिखती रहती हैं।

This story is published in Hindi, as sent by the reader. The English translation of the same is in the next chapter.

The Groom's Bus - by Pramod Verma

I was returning home from work, and just then my bike decided to break down midway. It was a dark and gloomy winter night with the sun disappearing pretty early in the evening. As my route was hitting a dense forest, I decided to take help from a crowded bus heading my way that seemed to be a wedding procession from the groom's side. I boarded the bus and saw the people inside it were comparatively dull instead of being chirpy about the wedding.

It was a full moon night and neither the bus driver nor the groom's men had uttered a single word throughout the drive. I found it odd and decided to part my way and take a taxi home. Suddenly, the bus started to drive in a chaotic manner, with people flying off from their seats, and it came to a halt by hitting a tree. I had hit my head really bad, and my arms were bruised badly, as I headed to the nearest highway, to get a taxi to head home.

I got into the taxi and started narrating my experience about this weird groom's bus, and suddenly the Taxi driver was taken aback and looked at me as if he had seen a ghost. He told me that a couple of years back the groom's bus had met with a tragic accident, where all the people on the bus including the groom were found dead after the bus lost control and fell into a steep hill. After which every year at the same time, the same bus haunts with the same people sitting alongside the groom, to then be seen by very few people as it goes and meets with the same accident where all of them vanish into the dense fog of death and darkness.

I couldn't believe my ears, and was thankful to my fortune, that I saved myself from the deadly plight of onboarding the bus that had people from the other world.

This story is English translation, and a modified version of the previous story published in Hindi.

The Flatmate - by Radhika Gupta

When I came to Delhi for business, I rented a flat to live in. There was a balcony in the bedroom of that flat. In front of that balcony was a house that was closed for many years. One day when I came home, I saw a 15 year old girl standing at the roof of that house. I panicked and asked her where she was from and what she was doing on the roof of the house at that hour of night. By the time I completed my questions, the girl jumped off the roof.

I ran downstairs barefoot and started to alarm everyone to gather around, as a girl had fallen from the roof. As I reached downstairs, to my surprise there was no girl, and everyone annoyingly looked at me to bother their sleep. The watchman told me that I might have seen the girl who had died many years back. As she was in love with a boy then and as her family refused, she had jumped off the roof and killed herself. After that incident her family had moved to their village and their apartment was kept closed without renting out to anyone else as that girl still haunted that place, sometimes at nights scaring away the dwellers.

Hungry - by Raghu

It was late, and I was exhausted from a grueling day of back-to-back meetings, endless discussions that led nowhere, and the usual blame games. When I entered the house, something felt off. The place was a mess; sweaty, dirty clothes were strewn everywhere. I didn't care much about it, then I suddenly realized I hadn't locked my car, so I peered through the window, hearing the faint "tink tink" of the remote as I locked it in the rain.

I tossed my bag into the corner and let my body collapse onto the bed. After downing a glass of water, I grabbed my phone to check for messages. There was a missed call from my flat mate, Vijay. He'd gone to his hometown that day, probably enjoying his parents' care and home food. My eyes were heavy, and once I set my phone on the table, I fell into a deep, much-needed sleep.

But it didn't last long. Restlessness took over. I tossed and turned, trying to find the right position, but something felt wrong. I got up and went to the bathroom. After relieving myself, I washed my face. Suddenly, the bathroom door slammed shut. An eerie sound echoed from above. Slowly, I looked up at the ceiling and saw a man crouching in the corner, poised to jump down. His face was completely distorted and bleeding. I could barely recognize that it was Vijay.

The lights flickered off, and I heard a thud as something landed behind me. Cold hands gripped my shoulders, turning me violently. "Ohhh... faaa!" I gasped as I jolted awake, my breath caught in my throat. It was just a nightmare, but a horrible one. My phone read 1:12 AM. I pulled the blanket over my head, trying to shut out fear.

Sleep eluded me. In an attempt to calm my nerves, I plugged in my earbuds and played the Hanuman Chalisa. Staring around the room, I finally drifted off, but not for long. I was startled awake by the sound of Vijay's voice calling me from the door. Confused, I thought he might've returned home, but why so late? I hesitated, I thought why am I still single, at least would have a supporting hand. The knocks grew louder, urging me to investigate.

I grabbed a bat from the corner and crept to the door. When I opened it, no one was there. But then, a low growl echoed from my room. I turned back to see a shadow, something twelve feet tall, bent and creeping toward me. The growl intensified. My mind screamed "Run!!!"

I sprinted for the door, only to come face-to-face with a monstrous version of Vijay. His head, grotesquely oversized, filled the entire doorway as he tried to squeeze through. Paralyzed, I swung the bat at him, but it made no difference. Another hand, massive and disfigured, reached for me from the archway. I stumbled over spilled water on the floor and fell. I woke up, gasping. Another nightmare.

At that moment, it hit me, I knew what was going on. My body was rebelling. I hadn't eaten dinner because of work, and my stomach had been torturing me all night. I dashed to the kitchen, rummaging through the cabinets. The only thing I could find was milk. I gulped down two Snickers bars and a large cup of tea. Finally, my stomach was content, and my mind relaxed. "Amma always said, 'Never sleep on an empty stomach.' Turns out, she was right," I muttered, chuckling to myself. Feeling lighter, I lay on the couch and fell into the deepest sleep I'd had in days.

The morning sunlight streamed through the window, waking me up. Refreshed, I turned on the radio and wandered around the house. Something nagged me, though, Vijay's room was locked. Odd, since he never locked it unless he was inside. Curiosity got better of me. I opened the door. And there he was, hanging from the fan.

Hitchhiker - by Dipannita Roy

Couple of years back, during the monsoon season, I and my friends had made plans to visit Kalapani Region(Nepal Border). It was raining heavily, and we decided for our first day to visit Pashupati market in Nepal. The roads had become foggy, as we started to head back to our hotel. We had a rental car and a local driver booked for this trip. The fog was dense and was covering the hilly roads like a thick layer, making it impossible to see anything outside of the car windows, as it had started to pour heavily.

Our driver, being a local dweller, started to head back slowly and carefully through the steep and slippery road. The road was empty covered with tall pine trees, and the forest adjacent to the road was pitch dark. After a few miles, we saw a lady standing by the side of the road asking for us to stop, her face covered with a white linen scarf, she seemed to be in distress, and we agreed to help. Soon after she sat, one of my friends started to ask her about her whereabouts. The air inside the car had turned a bit chilly, compared to earlier and I could smell a peculiar odor, and had started to feel sick. The driver started talking in his native language, to try his luck, but she didn't say much.

Suddenly the headlights went off, and sensing the ambiguous road ahead, the driver pushed the brakes, we all jumped from our seats with the jerk. My friend lit the flashlight from her cell phone, and we saw the woman's face right in front of us, turned 360 direction and having no eyes, nose just a mouth that was open to a black hole. We all screamed loudly, and she dropped her phone shaking profusely. We could all soon see her standing in front of the car and walking towards the dark forest. Our driver started the car and drove the whole way without headlights, until we reached the hotel safely.

An Asylum of the Walking Dead - by Anshu Habibi

I hail from Murshidabad in Bengal. My story begins during the wedding of my tutor, where I stayed for three days. A mental hospital stood ominously close to her house. She repeatedly warned me to disregard any unusual noises or occurrences, but one afternoon, I stepped out onto her balcony, shirtless.

Returning to the room, I fell asleep alone. Around 1 AM, a sound jolted me awake. In the dim moonlight, I saw a figure standing near my bed. The man's face was a grotesque mask of blood and scratches, and saliva dripped from his lips. I feigned sleep, terrified as he watched me with unsettling intensity.

Suddenly, he vanished. But a chilling sensation washed over me. I felt a presence behind me, breathing heavily and making guttural sounds. I was paralyzed with fear, unable to move. Desperate, I began chanting the Hanuman Chalisa, my voice trembling.

The morning call to prayer, the Azaan, finally broke the spell. The presence was gone. I immediately contacted my relatives and family, my blood running cold when they revealed the chilling history of the hospital: a place where thousands of tormented souls had met their demise.

The Power of a True Spirit - by Siddharth Singh

A house gets built on top of many other houses that have been built and torn apart. A new house has a lot of sentiments and mixed feelings about who used to live before them, what were their stories. Some maybe happy, most of them tragic, as life soon has death that follows. One such story is about a teenage girl, who was visiting her uncle, as there was a housewarming party.

Their house was newly constructed in a land bigger than her small cottage closer to the pond, filled with fishes, back in the village of Jagatsinghpur, Odisha. There is an old belief that when a house is constructed, no one alone should sleep in the house until after the rituals to cleanse the corners of each room with spiritual essence. So that if there are any spirits of other dimensions haunting the land they make their way to freedom or shift themselves to another location. Now the uncle's current house was comparatively compact, and the aunty was not too much onboard on accommodating a lot of guests at her place. So, they finally decided to sleep at the new house just the night before the housewarming party.

As they all fell sleep, this girl hears a knock and is asked by her aunt to go and open the door, not realizing it was almost after midnight. While she heads that way, she feels uncomfortable as she finds everyone in sidhe household sleeping, except her. When she opened the door, she found a woman with long hair and a red saree, looking at her, asking her questions about the house at that odd hour of night. The woman seemed normal, but something was off.

Now this girl was Lord Hanuman's disciple. She used to pray day and night chanting hymns of the powerful monkey god, Lord Hanuman. When she ended her conversation and lock the door, a shrill voice from the other side of the door warned her that because Lord Hanuman was standing right next to her, she was unable to snatch her eyes away. That woman was an age-old witch, haunting the site that night.

Jokha - by Elysian

It was the witching hour, 1:00 AM, in Raghurajpur, a village famed for the art of Pattachitra, when my grandma, along with a fellow villager, embarked on a bone-chilling journey. Their destination: the Kali Puja nearby, but their path, a shortcut through the jungle, was shrouded in an inky blackness, pierced only by their flickering oil lamp. The air hung heavy, thick with the cloying scent of decay and the unsettling silence broken only by the occasional rustle in the unseen undergrowth.

Looking ahead, a dilapidated palace, a skeletal silhouette against the starless sky, whispered of a bygone era of opulence. It was here, amidst the crumbling grandeur, that they spotted a flicker of light in the distance. Relief washed over them, perhaps other devotees on their way to the puja.

As they drew closer, a surge of primal terror coursed through their veins. The light emanated not from a fellow pilgrim, but from a creature of nightmare. A monstrous entity, a giant fireball with no eyes, pulsed with an unnatural light. Its grotesque form, a hideous fusion of molten rock and flickering flame, sent shivers down their spines.

Transfixed by the horrifying apparition, my grandma became a petrified statue. Time seemed to lose all meaning as she stood there, bathed in the creature's blinding light. It was then that her friend, hidden behind a gnarled tree, made a desperate gamble. With a grimace of repulsion, they doused the Jokha*, as these creatures were called, with urine.

A bloodcurdling shriek, unlike anything heard by man or beast, erupted from the creature as it recoiled. It lashed out in its fury, but its fiery tendrils dissipated harmlessly before reaching them. With a final, earsplitting growl, the Jokha vanished into the inky depths of the jungle.

Shaken to their core, they stumbled back towards the village, their hearts hammering a frantic tattoo against their ribs. But amidst the terror, a glimpse of gold caught their eye. Nestled beneath a crumbling stone, lay a cache of coins, a forgotten treasure guarded by the Jokha.

The urge to claim their spoils was strong, but a primal instinct for survival held them back. The Jokha might have retreated, but they knew the legend – these creatures were fiercely protective of their treasures. Taking anything would surely unleash its wrath once more.

Leaving the riches undisturbed, they fled back to the village, the chilling memory of the Jokha forever etched in their minds. They returned home, not as triumphant treasure hunters, but as survivors, forever haunted by the night they encountered the guardian of the damned.

Jokha is a mythical creature in Odia folklore, known to guard ancient treasures.

www.ingramcontent.com/pod-product-compliance
Lightning Source LLC
Chambersburg PA
CBHW061430160726
47995CB00003B/834